Curving Road

ILLINOIS SHORT FICTION

Other titles in the series:

Curving Road

Stories by John Stewart

UNIVERSITY OF ILLINOIS PRESS

Urbana   Chicago   London

"Blues for Pablo," *Stanford Short Stories, 1962,* ed. Wallace Stegner and
Richard Scowcroft (Stanford University Press).

Library of Congress Cataloging in Publication Data

Stewart, John, 1933
   Curving road.

   (Illinois short fiction)
   CONTENTS: Branches: Blues for Pablo.—The stretch:
Letter to a would-be prostitute. The pre-jail party.
[etc.]
   I.   Title.
PZ4.S8518Cu   [PS3569.T465]   813   75-2286
ISBN 0-252-00517-1
ISBN 0-252-00532-5 pbk.

To my Wife, my Mother, the Other Women—
who all guided my becoming

Contents

The Afomo has no roots; it claims relationship with every tree.
—Yoruba proverb

Branches

Blues for Pablo

Pablo had left his house at dawn that Thursday morning. He watched them kill four animals, stood by while they skinned the carcasses and emptied the hot entrails. In the dimly lit slaughterhouse where no foreign sound penetrated the thick walls save the churn of the outside refrigerating unit, his four men worked deliberately, jointing the dead bodies with precise movements, first into huge sides of beef, then into lesser and lesser cuts. There was not much talk amidst the hacking sounds of hatchet and knife, the piercing scrape of the saw. When they spoke they used only short, sharp grunts, and they seldom looked at each other. They were good men. Like himself, they were Mexicans, and often Pablo felt like a father to them. With age he had grown heavy and slow, but they were young. They moved lightly, and with a seriousness that matched the meticulous black hair gummed down above their bloody white coats. When he took the knife and prepared to open his finger they all stopped, standing where they were with the heavy darkness in their eyes, silently joining him in the sacred moment as the blood fell in slow, thick drops onto the sawdust floor. After he wiped the knife they resumed working, their feet stirring the flakes, making his blood one with that of the dead animals and when he was ready to leave, most of the beef already hung in cuts from the sharp iron hooks.

The sun was bright and hot as he emerged through the heavy doors, and as he started across the valley sweat began to form in slow drops all over his heavy face. The sweat came faster as he crossed over the railway tracks, walked under the freeway, and headed for the cluster of houses. There was not much shade from the afternoon sun. The houses rose square and low, their shadows lost against their own walls, and the scattered trees stood spare, dry from the summer heat. All along the narrow deserted streets across the valley he felt the finger throbbing with each pulse. It was a good feeling. It kept alive the moment when the knife had sliced in a quick, sharp pain to let the blood drip slowly down. That was a good moment. He gave, he did not lose. Each week he gave a few drops of blood, a little in gratefulness, a little to let their spirits know how great was his respect for the proud animals, but mostly to stir his own spirit into a strong compassion for everything alive.

His thick face impassively set in an unchanging expression, Pablo walked across the corner of City Terrace Drive with solid steps, admitting no vision of the old men sunning themselves on the bus-stop bench, the children with their dogs noisily prancing between the bakery and the store. He walked directly into the little library, and though he sweated freely, made no effort to stop the drops slipping from beneath his hat, streaking his dust-covered face.

"How are you today, Mr. Montez?" the lady clerk asked, not waiting to hear his answer, but going back between the shelves to return with the book. "We have a new one in," she said when she came back. "It's all about the last hours before he died. What a remarkable man! Would you like to have it?"

Pablo considered for several moments. He had no wish to disturb the ceremony of Thursday with new things, although something new was already introduced into his day. Shortly he would have to face the girl and her friend. "No," he said, shaking his head more than saying the word. The regular book with its smooth brown cover was part of Thursday. He liked the naked sword on the cover with the red cloth lapped over it. The slightly curved blade recalled a memory of days older than he himself, older than his father or grandfather. It produced visions of fierce naked men caked with sweat and dust receiving similar blades in their proud chests, fearlessly falling in the hot trampled sand, letting go life without a cry while their blood trickled red along the blade. Manolete was such a man. A man's life was only a preparation for the end of living, and when his end came, that torero let go fearlessly. Each week, through Manolete, Pablo reminded himself of his own fearlessness.

His finger still throbbed a little where the blood had dried in the narrow slit, and the clerk had already filled out the card when Pablo said, "Senora, could I take the book with me?"

"Oh yes, of course. Prefer to read at home today?" She smiled, fixing her glasses. "My, you must know this book by heart by now." She started making another card. "Where is your friend, the young girl? She never comes in anymore."

"She is perhaps in school," Pablo said. The lady clerk had seen the friendship start, had often watched them mount the hill together, and as she kept pushing the glasses back on her nose, her face showed a readiness to discover his secrets.

In City Terrace Heights people were always ready to find out secrets, especially his. For all of his five years on the hill Pablo had managed to keep them at a distance and had, like his house, become an attraction. On the streets he could see the women stop and look, and he knew they talked of him. When he passed on, they'd turn and point at his house and go on talking—not the young ones, but the old wrinkled women who met to gossip when the evenings were warm. They were all Mexicans too, the people in the streets and the people in the little white houses, but he didn't know them and he had no wish to know them. The curious ones wanted to know him— like the lady clerk behind her glasses. He knew they talked about him and the girl; she didn't care, and Pablo didn't care either, except he wanted them to leave her alone, as they left him alone.

Leaving the library, Pablo walked to the broken old Jew selling papers across the street. Nobody talked about the Jew, nobody ever pointed at him, but he too was a proud man. As Pablo approached, the Jew left the narrow shade cast by his cardboard stand. His eyes seemed the only nourished things about his thin, sunken face and they glittered strongly as he came out to meet Pablo. With all Pablo felt for the humped man in the baggy suit and greasy cap, there was no need for words. Pablo paid slowly for his paper, they shook hands, and the Jew turned back to his scanty shade.

Pablo went through the motions of Thursday with his usual heaviness. After getting the paper, he went to the store. He stepped right by the old men gathered on the bus-stop bench who were not waiting for any bus. Most of them were as dark as he, but they were bony and wrinkled. They were not as broken as the Jew, and they were not as proud. They sat switching the flies away, talking rapidly, while the wine bottle in a brown paper sack passed from hand to hand. They paid him no attention, and he paid them none. It was all the same for them. He felt a different compassion—they would all die wrong. They would dry up and die. They would have no blood to give and the spirits would remain asleep when they died. Pablo bought the wine and started home.

So far Thursday had gone as usual. He'd given his blood, he'd got the book, and he'd got the paper and wine. But as he drew nearer the house, the presence of the girl came down to meet him, and he could no longer put off thinking of the strange situation into which she had placed him.

It seemed a long time since the day when she had smiled and they had spoken for the first time. Before that, she used to be the unknown virgin of his Thursdays, because each time he went to the library she was there, her round face always intent over an open book. She wore her black hair loose, and it fell over her sweater, almost down to her waist. She was always in sweaters and skirts, and when they first met, her legs were covered with long socks. As Pablo thought of what she looked like in those days, he realized it was not even a year ago when she seemed such a child. She had later told him it was all because she had heard the women in the library talking about him, but the first time she spoke, she'd waited for him to come out and said, "Isn't it odd, our meeting at the library every Thursday?" In those days Pablo read his book at the library. He never brought it home. It was not easy to think of something to say, and he'd asked why did she come to the little place; the college must have a bigger library.

"I like the atmosphere," she'd replied. "When I walk down City Terrace, it's like being in Mexico. Of course I've never been there, but I have a feeling for the place. You know, when I sit near the window and watch all the Mexicans passing up and down—it's tremendously different from campus. It's like being in an entirely foreign country."

"For you, then, Mexico is a land of mystery?"

"Well, sort of. But I am sure I would like it. I like you. You are very Americanized, but I like you."

She was so simple then. So easily she said, "I like you," that Pablo had felt a great elation for many days afterwards, even though he only half-believed her. With his greater years he knew liking someone was not such a simple thing. But she'd said it again when she came to the house. She was studying Spanish, and when she came they pretended not to know any English until he grew tired of her great accent and said it was too hard for him to remember so much Spanish. He offered her wine, and they drank. Then she came every Thursday, and after the Spanish, they'd drink wine and she would talk. It was nice to have her in the house. She was young and quick, and sometimes when she would sit as quietly as he for a long time, he could feel all the strain of the words she was holding back. It was good to feel that she did this for him. Everything was good, and the night when she came up through the rain there was nothing to do but to take her in.

It was a Thursday night. When he opened the door she stood holding a suitcase in one hand and some books in the other, with a few wet hairs sticking to her face and the skirt wrapped tight around her young legs. She had waited with a question on her face, until he'd motioned her in.

"It's cold outside," she said.

"Where are you going?" he asked, when he already knew the answer.

She grinned, "I've been put out. I've been put out in the rain. Can you imagine that?"

"Who would put you into the rain?"

He'd had visions of an angry father, or a mother who heard she came to his house, and when she said, "My friend," he'd suddenly realized that all the time he didn't know where she lived, or much else about her, except that she went to the college and came to his place every Thursday. When he found out her "friend" was the third man with whom she had lived it was a slight shock.

"Your friend, he doesn't want you anymore?"

"Well, actually, he wants to do as he pleases with me. I must come when he wants me to come and go when he wants me to go. I'm not his servant." She seemed to be enjoying being able to say that, and when she asked, "You don't mind my coming here, do you?" there was in her voice something which said she'd enjoy it just as much to say she wasn't his servant.

Yet in their five months together she was mostly very kind. She did strange things sometimes, and said even stranger things, but she'd brought something to the house that was never there before. From the first, she treated the house as though she'd known it all her life. She used it as he himself never had. She had books, and at night she used all the lights. She left her things, combs, hairpins, sometimes her clothes, wherever she dropped them, and always Pablo had to clean the kitchen after she cooked. But it was a special happiness to have her there—to see her leave on mornings with the books under her arms, and to have her come home on evenings, flinging things down, and kicking her shoes off. They were like father and daughter for weeks, until one day they touched and he wanted to be her fourth man. After that happened, she said, "You're such a man. You've made me learn to love, Pablo, do you realize that? I'll never forget you."

At a curve in the up-winding road, Pablo stopped. The sun stabbed steadily at his back, and in his narrow hat he cast a stunted shadow that barely slipped over the road into the sandy bank. The dust still came, some of it floating higher, much of it falling on the short, dry grass that ran straggling back from the road. Ahead, the avocado tree, partly covered with dust also, waved thick branches outside the kitchen window. He was high up, and he looked steadily at the house above, but couldn't see if anyone was watching down. After he'd rested, Pablo took his eyes away, and gazing only at the loose dirt road, he started up the last steep rise trying not to breathe too heavily.

She was young and her tricks were sometimes very simple, but there were things about Rhoda that Pablo couldn't quite explain: like when her face said one thing and her body said another. She had several faces. Sometimes she was the smiling college girl; at other times she looked like a hard whore; or sometimes she could be as innocent as a virgin. In the beginning she had only one face, and after he became her man they spoke mostly with their bodies. That was sufficient. Pablo couldn't remember when the faces started, but with their coming a restlessness came to the house, and it showed sometimes in the way she talked.

"Where do you go every Thursday, Pablo?"

"I go to see my men. The men who work for me."

"You never told me you had men working for you." He'd remained silent. "Why don't you ever talk? I swear, it's always a pain to get anything out of you."

"You will not like to hear what my men do."

"What do they do?"

"They kill the bulls."

"Kill bulls! You mean in a bullfight?"

"Oh no, in my slaughterhouse."

"You have a slaughterhouse? My God! I don't know what I'll find out about you next."

It was night while they talked, and Pablo had felt the distance grow between them on the bed. He talked about himself, hoping that what he said would bring her back nearer. He told her of the blood he gave each Thursday, about the book, and the paper, and the wine.

She was very curious. "Why do you read the same book over and over again?"

"He was a great man. He lived by the spirits, and when he died, his place with the greatest spirits was already waiting."

"Is that what you want to do? I mean when you die? I mean, is that what you want to happen to you when you die?"

"I already have a place. I have only to keep it."

"And that's what the blood's for?"

"Yes."

"But what do the paper and wine have to do with it?"

"The paper has nothing to do with it, except I buy from a Jew who is also a spiritual man. And the wine, it is nothing but wine. I drink, and feel happy that I am alive, and that I know where I am going when I die."

"You're such a man!" she'd exclaimed. She had come back nearer to him, Pablo could feel, even though her next words were hardly what he expected.

"Pablo, would you mind if I go to bed with other men?"

He'd grunted, neither yes nor no, because he was trying to understand what she wanted and to think what was good for her.

"I knew you wouldn't mind. You're such a man," she repeated. "I feel so free with you. Let us have an understanding, Pablo. If I have a man, I'll bring him here, and you can bring your women, too. I know you have other women; but that way there'll be nothing going on behind your back, nothing behind my back. And we can be real lovers." He'd grunted again, neither yes nor no. Sometimes she could be a woman, but that night she was a child.

He hadn't brought any women to the house; he hadn't needed any other women. Yet he wasn't very shocked when she said last night she was bringing a man to the house today. He was in his chair and she had come into his room. "I'm not really interested in him, I just think he'd be fun. Do you mind?" She was wearing her little girl's face. She held his hand and talked like a child reminding her father of a promise he'd made. He'd grunted, neither yes nor no, because there was nothing to say except he'd stay at the library all day.

But she said, "No, no. You must come home early, Pablo. You must be here."

The people in the valley all knew she lived there. They saw her through their windows each morning going down in her black skirt with books under her arm; and on evenings they saw her from their flat open porches as she came back. From their steps and streets they would see whoever the strange man was who came up the narrow road.

Yet while she'd held his hand, pretending they'd for the time become just good friends, he felt he should do or say something to make her see how ignorant it was to play the whore while he was there. But her little girl's face was ready to call him jealous, and he didn't know how to make her use the face that would understand.

When he reached the house there were voices. Pablo sat on the top step and took off his hat. He put down the things he carried, then wiped the dust and sweat from his face. Inside the house he heard them laughing—Rhoda in her girlish voice and the man with a not much heavier tone. The hill was quiet when their voices faded, except for the sound of traffic below and the wind through the avocado tree. The cars and people he could see over on College Hill were tiny figures shifting in the bright sun between the red buildings and square patches of green. Pablo wasn't jealous, and he wasn't hurt that she should be with another man in his house, but he still thought she was making a great waste of herself with her game of faces and men.

When he heard them again she was talking in the voice that matched her whore's face. Pablo was very hot and tired. His finger with the dried blood caked in its rings throbbed slightly, and he felt a little awkward about going in because the man sounded so young.

Suddenly the kitchen door behind him opened. "Pablo," she called, "Pablo, don't sit out there. Come inside and meet Eddie." He picked up the wine and book and left the paper on the step. She held the door open, and as he walked by, "Ah, you brought the book. You'll read while I talk with Eddie? But you must meet him first."

Like his voice, Eddie was slight, but firm. Not as dark as Pablo, his black hair fell heavy and straight, and his quick, easy movements as he left his seat made Pablo very aware of his own thickness. A constant smile tugged at the corners of Eddie's mouth all the while Rhoda was saying, "Eddie Pena, and this is Pablo . . . my roommate." She was smiling too as Eddie extended his slim hand. Pablo shook, slowly letting his eyes run over the young man again. Although he was slender, his muscles were well formed. He was perhaps no older than Rhoda, and he reminded Pablo very much of what he had looked like when he was young, except with his constant smile Eddie seemed more knowing than even Rhoda herself with her many faces. "Eddie's from Costa Rica," she was saying. "He's in my art class."

"So you are an artist?" Pablo asked.

"Eddie is a great artist," she said, bustling back into the kitchen. She wore the regular schoolgirl skirt and sweater, and her hair, braided in one long heavy pigtail, bounced down her back as she returned with the bottle of wine and glasses. The room was neater than usual. The regular heap of books and papers was cleared and the floor was swept clean of ashes. From the dusty window a streak of yellow sun ran the length of the room, and as they moved, the bare floor creaked slightly with every step. They took seats at the table, and Rhoda poured the wine. She kept the first glass for herself and offered the second to Pablo.

"No, Eddie," Pablo said, waving a hand at the young man.

"I do not drink, senor," Eddie said with a smile of satisfaction. Pablo took the wine and drank it in one draught. "This is a very nice house," the boy said.

"Well, not pretty, but a good house," Pablo answered. He wasn't sure how he should talk to Eddie, but wished only to let the boy know there were no bad feelings.

"He built it himself," Rhoda said.

"Is that right, senor?"

"Yes, little by little. I wanted to have more rooms, but it is big enough."

"He got tired and stopped," Rhoda said.

"With four rooms, that's plenty when you are alone, is it not, senor?"

"One of these days Pablo is going to get a wife and start having children. That's what he was thinking about," she said. Eddie's smile slipped into a polite laugh, but Pablo sat hunched in his chair not looking at the young man. "When are you going to get married, Eddie?" she asked.

"After a long time," he answered quickly. "After I've done something." He sat with the same ease Rhoda showed when she first came, an ease that Pablo couldn't feel with a strange man in the house.

"So you're an artist?" Pablo asked again.

"I told you," Rhoda said in her impatient girl's voice. "He's great."

"You paint?" Pablo asked.

"No, senor, I work with the clay," answered Eddie.

"He is a genius," she said. "You ought to see the crucifix he did."

"You did a crucifixion?" Pablo asked.

"A crucifix, senor. Christ hanging on the cross."

"You make a crucifixion out of clay?" Pablo said in his slow, heavy voice.

"He is a genius," she said again excitedly.

Pablo filled his glass from the bottle. "No, Eddie," he said. "A crucifixion out of clay, that is no good. Where is the blood?" The strong wine made his nose tingle, and Pablo drank until his glass was empty.

Eddie was saying, "The blood is in the clay. There was no cup under the cross, senor, all the blood fell into the ground." The boy was quick. Rhoda sat watching him with her whore's eyes and Pablo felt little beads of sweat form on his own face again. He didn't hate the young man. He felt only a little sorry that such a boy could know how to get behind Rhoda's faces. Eddie had neither his knowledge nor his experience, but in his own young way he had a means of finding her out that Pablo didn't have. He could hurt, but Pablo could only protect her.

"Don't you think he's great?" she asked.

Pablo grunted and took some more wine. He pondered, considering if there was any truth in what Eddie said, while the two talked freely. Soon he was out of the conversation. They turned to him only when she asked support for her exclamations about things she herself had told him and then he would nod or shake his head without looking at either of them directly until they started talking again. They argued over strange names, Degas, Goya, and others, Rhoda putting on her college face and Eddie with his face serious and sharp, although his eyes never stopped smiling. Taking his lead from Rhoda, Pablo felt he was acting quite well like a father and was on the point of leaving the room when she said, "Pablo too has a deep artistic sense. He never talks, but it is there. Perhaps the greatest artistic sense I've ever known."

"Is he too an aesthete?" Eddie asked with a challenge in his voice. "Where is his work?"

"He used to be a matador!" she exclaimed.

Pablo felt very satisfied when he saw the expression that brought to Eddie's face. He looked at Rhoda and she was watching him with all the expectancy of a little girl.

"Did you change your name, senor? I never heard of Pablo."

Putting down his glass slowly, Pablo said, "You are too young."

He had a strange feeling of contentment in being able to say so to Eddie with the girl listening. "In my work there is life and blood, not clay."

"Where did you enter the ring, senor?" the boy asked, still challenging.

"Mexico. I was born in Mexico." Pablo kept his voice even and deep, letting each word fall heavily into the room. "My first bull was in the great Plaza before thousands of people . . . when I too was young." He paused and the room was so quiet as the others waited that the hum of traffic from the distant freeway became noticeable. "But it is not nice the way people watch, the things they want from the fight. They see only the wrong things. You have been to the Plaza, Eddie?"

"Yes, senor," the boy said without lifting his face.

"What did you laugh at?"

"I do not laugh senor, but the whole thing is silly. The man kills the bull, the bull kills the man, it is only a game with death. You are a quiet man but lucky to be sitting here at all."

Pablo pushed back his chair and stood up. The desire to let Eddie know what an unlearned boy he was took possession of Pablo. He tried to hold the folds of his body tight, even though his stomach fell, and his loose breasts made sagging heaps under his wrinkled suit. But he looked down on Eddie, and with his serious face said, "Silly things we see through silly eyes. A wise bull is not easy to understand, and neither is a man, Eddie. When the two face, it is a strange thing that happens. A man killed, a bull killed, yes; but the blood of it is a sacred thing." From the corner of his eye Pablo could see Rhoda watching him with her young face, silently supporting him, but he didn't lower his eyes. He held himself up high as if in salutation to the fluttering trumpets of the Plaza, and went on. "Such a bull I had for my first time, Eddie, a wise bull. He knew I was not afraid. He was not afraid. And never once he came for the cloth; the body always. Low, with his eyes shut. Twice I moved, twice he came back faster. The third time I ran. They laughed, Eddie; you ever hear the whole Plaza laugh? They laughed because they thought I was a coward. The bull knew I was young. When he stood away from the barrera I saw him opening his black scornful eyes. To respect is not to be afraid, do you know that? You are a young man, but always remember, to respect is not to be afraid." Pablo stopped, and the traffic hum came again.

"You ran, senor?" Eddie asked quietly.

"Only the first time," replied Pablo from his height above the young man.

"You are a brave man," Eddie chuckled. "I admire you."

"Pablo is a brave man," Rhoda said, "like any great artist. It is the bravest thing I know for a man to cut himself each week."

"You cut yourself, senor?" Eddie asked, surprised and a little shocked.

"I give a little blood to the spirits. It is a small thing," Pablo said.

"He does," she said, "every Thursday at his own slaughterhouse."

"You keep a slaughterhouse?" Eddie asked with even greater surprise. "From a matador, you become a butcher, senor?"

"He doesn't kill," she said, "he just owns the place." They were both very quick, and talked with an ease that didn't have any dignity. Pablo put down his glass and picked up the book.

"You are a fine man, Senor Pablo. One day I will do you with my clay."

Pablo said nothing. He just left the room with all the stiff highness that he could manage.

"You will not need to cut yourself," Eddie called. "Remember already there is blood in my clay."

As Pablo left the two, he felt his finger throbbing slightly again, and for a short time it didn't matter that they were together, alone, free for Rhoda to make her faces with Eddie looking on like a smiling cat. He went to the bathroom and washed the brown dust from his skin and hair.

His own room had none of the yellow sun slanting through its bareness. The only decoration he had allowed himself was the parochial calendar nailed up above the bureau, with its lustful angel looking directly down at his bed. With a deliberate movement Pablo lifted the chair and placed it nearer the window. Then he sat down and, opening the book, started again at chapter four.

The torero was in the act of once more exhausting his third bull.

He called for the sword and wiped it clean through the red cloth. With a fearless step he marched back to the center of the ring surrounded by the screaming Plaza. Suddenly through the sweaty stink and dust, he saw the fierce ancestors tumbling, one after the other, their exposed breasts spotted with the flowing blood . . . voices came again, loudly, from her room this time.

She talked freely, as though he was not in the house, and when Eddie tried to make her speak more softly she said, "It doesn't matter if he hears. We have an understanding." Eddie murmured something again, and she said in her rasping whore's voice, "You let him frighten you with his pretending to be a matador?" Eddie murmured again, and she said, "Heavens, no. He gets that out of a book he reads every Thursday." Eddie murmured. "Oh yes, he cuts himself. Didn't you notice the finger he held away from his glass?" They talked on, her loud whore's voice answering Eddie's delicate murmurs. Pablo didn't wish to listen. It didn't matter if Eddie knew he was not a torero, he was in touch with the spirits—that made him as good as all toreros—but it was painful to hear her expose herself too easily. In her confiding in Eddie, she was really saying that he didn't have any right to protect her. It was very painful to hear her show Eddie how much she wished to be used. They fell silent, but the raspy words with which she'd answered Eddie's murmurs seemed to penetrate again and again into the room, blurring the vision of his mystic torero. He could no longer read, and his oneness with the bleeding ancestors was no longer real. Pablo stood up and looked out the window beyond which his house sent a dark shadow stretching up the hill. Quietly he pondered whether he should send them away or whether he should leave; but before he did either came the light swish of clothing, then all was quiet again, until the struggling moans began. Pablo didn't want to listen, but he couldn't trust himself to move because he was afraid his legs would carry him to her door. Then from the thick moans her little girl's voice cried out hoarsely, like a pig after its throat is cut. Again and again her cry sank into Pablo, but there was no sound from Eddie. The book fell. The feelings which ran through him moved much swifter than he could, and as her cries came faster and higher he lifted his heavy wounded hand and crashed it against the bureau. Blood squashed out of his finger, and after a moment, when the pain came warm and biting, he went back outside.

With his finger pulsing pain, Pablo sat again on the steps. From College Hill his eyes slipped down over the valley. Back among the grey warehouses was the cool, dim slaughterhouse with thick walls, and the sawdust floor that held his blood mingled with that of the bulls. Pablo picked it out. It was very far away, and seemed now to have no connection with his heavy, swollen finger stiff with the blood still sticky around the pulpy split. Down on City Terrace the old men still crowded on the bus-stop bench, and the Jew, quite small from where Pablo sat, still hopped about in front of his paper stand. The women were coming out now. One by one the low houses opened their doors, and out of their dark insides the women stepped, some with children on their hips, others walking idly with baskets; and when the sun finally slipped behind College Hill, the streets that were deserted when he crossed in the stinging afternoon heat were clustered with groups of dresses. If anyone had seen Eddie, the talk would spread, and they would wait, watching from below, guessing at what went on inside the house on the hillside.

Pablo made an army out of the great shadow of College Hill, starting its advance over the valley. Led by the tall college walls it inched on rapidly, covering the tracks and warehouses, climbing over City Terrace Avenue with its lounging men and gossiping women, moving steadily up his dust-smothered hill. It was a good army. It conquered without feeling, until all was grey. Shadows were not men, they had no weaknesses. But even as Pablo spurred the dusky march against daylight he still remembered Rhoda's wailing cries, felt still the terrible tenderness they'd opened in him.

She used to be beautiful, especially on mornings before her skin grew hot and the pimples made little red spots in her face. With her eyes then she could make his body lose its heaviness, snap hard, a firm support for her natural softness. Eddie had touched that softness, made her wail not in comfort but in fright. He couldn't hear what went on in her room from where he sat, but Pablo knew she must have cried like that several times over. Pablo didn't hate the young man, he just felt very sad that Rhoda was so easily free with the pitiful little girl cries, and for him had so many false faces.

He didn't hear them come until she said, "Isn't it beautiful?" When he looked around they were standing just behind him, and Rhoda with outstretched hand was pointing down at the valley, but Eddie's eyes were on him, smiling warmly with the contentment of a grateful guest. "Don't you think it's great?" she asked.

"It's very nice. You have an exquisite view here, Senor Pablo," Eddie said, still looking at Pablo, smiling.

"It's beautiful," she said again in her college girl's voice. "If you wait, you'll see how pretty it is when the lights come on." They weren't looking at the valley, they were looking at the college. "It's a great place," she said, talking with no hint of the crying wail in her voice.

"It is a nice place, but not great," Eddie said, and once again they argued in school-like voices, as if nothing had taken place in the bed next to Pablo's room. Even when she held Eddie's arm Pablo felt there was no private meaning in her touch. There was a hardness about both of them. Her hair was plaited tighter than before, and, like her breasts, her face pointed sharp and hard in the grey dusk. He turned his eyes away.

"Listen to the leaves," she said, "listen. Nothing on this hill whispers as tenderly as that. When I'm alone, I sit and pretend they're talking to me."

The young man laughed. "Do the leaves talk to you too, Senor Pablo?"

But before Pablo could answer she said, "He doesn't have any tenderness. He's strong, and he knows beauty, but he doesn't have any tenderness."

"How can he know beauty and not have tenderness?" Eddie asked.

"Gauguin was not a tender man," she said.

"You are wrong, senorita; in Gauguin there was such a heart, he felt tenderness for the most grotesque things . . ." They talked on. They ignored Pablo. Their voices went quickly, and they said many things about him as though he were not listening. He waited, and as they went back inside Eddie called, "You are a fine man, Senor Pablo. Next time I come I'll bring my clay." Pablo didn't hate the boy. He wanted Eddie to know that in his heart there was no hate.

He stood up to say good-bye, but before he turned, the door was closed behind them both. Pablo sat down again. He thought of the many times he'd held her body next to his—he didn't have many words, but there was tenderness in those times. He sat remembering fiercely how after a night together she would awaken with the morning light on her round face, and sometimes with a smile, but always wordlessly, slip out of bed to dress for school. There was never any hard talking with him; he had a respect for what their bodies found together, and while they lay still, the spirits always came and stood at a safe distance watching.

It had grown too dark for Pablo to see who was watching from below, but he knew there were people out in the warm streets watching Eddie as the boy bobbed down the hill, straight and blacker than the dark slope. Together she and the young man had laughed at him. He knew. They were young and fast, but they had never felt the hot pain of a knife and watched their blood run. They laughed at his imaginary bull, but she had never seen a bull die or smelled the hot insides as they were emptied out. A man was not much different. The low houses had already lighted up their square windows, and Pablo watched until Eddie disappeared toward the foot of the hill. He couldn't hear her stirring, but he waited, half hoping she would join him on the step. When after some time she didn't, Pablo went in.

She was seated at the table with one of her books opened beside the half-empty wine bottle. She didn't look up, and Pablo remained in the kitchen. After a few moments he found that he was hungry, but when he started to get out meat for dinner she left the table saying, "Don't Pablo, I'll cook dinner." She gripped the saucepan that he held, but he didn't let it go immediately.

She let her hand fall and said, "Are you angry with me?"

Pablo grunted and shook his head. He wasn't sure what he felt about her.

She held his sleeve and spoke with her little girl face, "Did you like Eddie?" Pablo didn't answer. "What's the matter with you?" she asked. Pablo put down the saucepan and she followed him into the living room. "What's the matter? Did I do something wrong?"

"Do you like Eddie?" he asked.

"Why, I don't know—it's not a matter of liking him. Is that

what's worrying you? Why don't you say what's worrying you?"

"He is very hard," Pablo said.

"Well, what do you think I am?"

She had looked hard out in the grey light, but now that Eddie was gone her face and breasts no longer pointed like sharp rocks. Pablo searched for what he wanted to say. "You are soft. Inside you are very soft." That wasn't really what he meant. She laughed. "Eddie . . . is not good for you." It was very difficult to say what he had in mind.

"You're jealous," she burst out, "Pablo, you're jealous."

"Together we have been with the greatest spirits."

She refused to understand. "I never thought I could make you jealous."

"That is for children," Pablo snapped. "A man is never jealous."

"Then what are you talking about?"

"I heard you cry out. Eddie hurt you."

"I always cry like that. Eddie can't hurt me . . . besides, what were you doing listening to the cries I made?"

"You're a child. You do not know what you are doing."

"If all you have to do is listen to what goes on in my room then all I can say is I'm ashamed for you."

"I was not listening. I heard."

"Such an old ass . . . do you know what you're doing? You with your phony toreros and your bleeding finger? You don't fool me." Her breasts went up and down quickly, and there was no falseness in her shining face. "What are you trying to do, put me out? Well I can go. I'll find a place." She went to her room.

Where Pablo stood was filled with the smell of open wine; it was warm inside the house, and the freeway noise came like a steady drone. Yet already the place seemed empty. It was a heavy thing to do, but after a few moments Pablo followed her.

The door was open, and she sat on the bed with her knees together, her chin propped on her hands. As he approached, she looked up and he stopped. There were things he wanted to say, but they were hard to find.

She spoke first.

"Do you love me, Pablo?" He could only stand silently watching her. She came to her feet. "You never tell me, Pablo—you never tell me anything. Why don't you talk?"

He remembered how quickly she and Eddie could talk. "Words don't come quickly when a man's old."

She came to him. "But I'm very young, Pablo. Would you forgive me if I'm very young sometimes?"

He put his arms around her, and she gave in against him.

"We can talk without words, can't we, Pablo?"

He grunted softly.

After he had supported her for a few moments she said, "Pablo, when will we go to Mexico? I want to see real bulls. You always say they are so beautiful . . . let's see them together, alive and real . . . and a real torero."

"You are very ignorant," he said.

"I know, I know. I am so stupid. Remember the first time how you had to hold my arms . . . you made me so helpless."

Pablo remembered well. She was never helpless. She had fought hard like a wild dog, until he was sweating and tired. Then she had said she didn't mean to fight. But there was nothing really hard about her as she leaned on him. He was much harder.

"You could be so strong," she said, starting to rub her body against his.

The Stretch

Letter to a Would-be Prostitute

January 1969

Sister:

Your letter came in time for Xmas, and I would like to say I had to think long and deeply so that I could make a decent response. But really, it was just my laziness in waiting for the "right mood" that kept me so long from answering. I remember how terrible our winter in New York was after it had become clear our affair would not survive, and I am sorry you are undergoing a similar torture again. Yet, this time, the sacrifice you so desperately seek to escape is shared by thousands of women like yourself—young, lonely, restless, awaiting word from someone in Viet Nam—and even though there is little comfort to be found in strange numbers, if enough of us bend our wills to surviving trying times creatively, the phenomena of individual failures and quasi suicidal acts will disappear from the face of the earth.

I cannot applaud your inclination to drop your career with the social agency and become a prostitute—exhausting as it might be, being entertained by those shallow unhappy men in search of pleasure; lonely and depressing as it is not hearing from Clyde and having no panaceas for the destitute in Harlem. I still believe that love is one of the best productive forces in the world. And while a dead lover may make way for a new lover, the men who buy prostitutes are not lovers. What does prostitution produce? What are its rewards? Does it really make anybody happy? At best, I believe, prostitution gives deadly encouragement—from the point of view of the prostitute—to our propensity for surrendering instead of struggling, and for attaching false values to self-defeat. Let me tell a story that will, I hope, illustrate what I mean.

You will recall that when Mike and I left New York for California in 1966 we had a new car, some credit cards, and a few friends it would be nice to pay surprise visits to along the way. We took Highway 80 west, and driving for the sheer pleasure of going swept through New Jersey, Pennsylvania, Ohio, Indiana, Illinois, stopping only to gas up and eat. After we left the town of Davenport on the Mississippi in eastern Iowa, we started going over the people we wanted to see in Iowa City. There were Al, and Chet, and two others whom I did not know—special friends of Mike's—and the professor. What made us think of the professor? He had never been particularly Mike's friend, nor mine. In all the years spent between us at the university we could remember no more than two occasions on which he and one of us had sat at the same beer-drinking table. What made us think of him? You must know Iowa City to understand. It is a city inhabited by people who cling jealously to certain pioneering instincts. They are distrustful and suspicious of strangers. Like the "primitive" bands one may read about, which regard outsiders as witches bearing strange and dangerous sorcery. And, in the style of such bands, they often adopt offense as the best means of protection against envisaged harm. The stranger in Iowa City is fair game for hairy-faced old women and bantam yokels alike. And it doesn't stop there. Among themselves, the merchant and the farmer, the mechanic, the doctor, the banker, all know that each is out to succor himself at the expense of the other, and the barrage of tricks with which they surround themselves from a stranger is ten times multiplied, resharpened, in their specific daily combats with each other. The innocent smile, handshake, offer of a drink, are often not innocent at all, but deadly moves in a game you don't even know they are playing.

I recall, for instance, a man who used to go around the world soliciting young artists to come to his shop in Iowa to develop their talents. He offered them money, a place to work, the company of other young artists. And when you got there this was all true—there was money, a place to work, and other young talent—only at the last moment you were told you had to say "oink" before you got any of it. And sometimes you were never even given that chance. You were consigned right off—depending upon the degree of your destitution —to the peonage of his fraternal system. You, figuratively, swept the shop, shoveled the stables, fed the animals, and did many other menial jobs on a dole that kept you in coffee and doughnuts and an occasional hamburger—if you watched the cigarettes. It took us a long time to discover that this man was, perhaps unconsciously, bent on hamstringing all the artists he could lay hands on in our age group. But that is another story: not the one I want now to tell.

So as I said, you must understand Iowa City for the peculiar place it is, with hostilities and animosities and to-the-death petty competitions as the natural pathways along which people move to reckon up their relationships. Then imagine Mike and me seeking our growth in such a place. Imagine any young black man seeking his growth in such a place—where people didn't admit they found you phobic, but granted you the favor of recommending rooms in Goat Hollow; where there were no serious community problems except a few thousand alcoholics; where there was no rampant sickness except that which made people lock their doors against others stranded during blizzards; where on a stroll during late spring nights you could expect white boys stacked up in humming automobiles to stick their heads out the windows shouting NIGGER! You will understand why it was in Iowa City that we learned to steal and brawl, why for long stretches at a time we suspended connections with our humanity and pretended to be iron men in physical and mental constitution (never mind the moral) out-savaging the savages. And why did we want to go back to such a place after three years? The question is still with me: I have no answer.

But see us on an early spring evening sixteen and a half hours out of New York, the car running fine, us at ease with ourselves, our old hostilities practically all forgotten, on the road—and you know how the road used to symbolize freedom to us black men—leaving the little river town of Davenport, going west to a familiar place sixty miles up ahead. The sun going down, and everywhere with the last

snow gone, the dry fields busy, you could tell—despite the cold wind
and coming night—brewing up a new year's life. The leafless trees
vowing that next time seen they would be shaking green, and the sky
placid in grey-blue triumph over the dying winter. We would probably have considered going to see the devil that evening if he were
within reach. No pun on the professor here, no metaphor intended.
Our minds, centered as they were upon pleasant memories associated with the season, remembered him as a generous man who had offered us rooms in which to sleep during our earliest days in that
hostile land. We remembered him as a man leading picket lines
against the town barbershops that had refused to cut Negro hair. A
socialist talking about open housing, and other "radical reforms,"
his photograph used to be in every evening's newspaper, followed by
pages of irate letters to the editor and petitions to the governor to
send down investigating committees. And in those days any man
who got his name in the press for advocating social reform was auto-
matically a friend to us. Especially when he could recite, as the professor often did, from *The Fire Next Time*. See us, then, high on
"Alabama" which we had whistled all the way from New York with
aside from Al, Chet, and Mike's two special friends, this professor—
a man of ideals and commitments with which we identified—the
only other person in our memory from university days. He was least
on the list, and so we decided to visit him first.

When we came to Iowa City we crossed the second of three bridges
leading off the highway, cruised through town, then drove alongside
the river up to the professor's address. A word about this river. It
runs through the center of town, and is a tributary of the Mississippi.
At one time, they say, during the days when the first white pioneers
settled here, the river was a main water link to other parts of the
country, and bore much traffic of hunters, trappers, robbers,
Indians, etc. But it is now only a decoration. The grassy banks are
themselves bordered with low-trimmed hedges, and above the
hedges, trees. Everywhere trees—birch, beech, catalpa, and many
others the names of which I never stopped to learn—still leafless that
evening, and silent, seemingly unconcerned with protecting the ele-
gant residences between them. While we followed this river to the
professor's house a tree here, a patch of lawn there reminded me

strongly of my own romantic interludes in this city, time back when every plump crotch seemed indeed the pathway to salvation. But it is not my intention to talk about that either.

At last we came to the white two-story house with its colonial facade, and Mike rang the bell. The professor and his wife were reading in their separate leather chairs when the maid let us in. They did not seem much changed. His face was still clear and ruddy, his eyes brightly focused, grey-streaked hair well groomed in a flowing pompadour. His clothes were still casual Ivy League, but when he greeted us there was something wary about his manner that made me uneasy. His wife was a year older than he, but looked also very trim in tweed slacks and a cotton shirt which she didn't bother to button up against the early wrinkles between her breasts. She ignored our hands and kissed us, saying how marvelous it was to see us again. "Won't you sit down? Have a drink. You are just a little late for dinner, but you may have anything you like to drink. The house is well stocked." We sat down with drinks in our hands, but the atmosphere was frosty.

"How was New York?" the professor asked.

So how was it? We had stories to tell about our jobs at that school for so-called crazy young boys—most of them spirit-broken before eleven, already jaded on the amusements of their genitals. Sweet boys. Destitute boys. Who could make cotton a difficult thing to wear and sugar a bitter thing to taste, because of the history of lost ancestral blood upon Southern plantations, this loss manifest in the trials they endured as pawns in another New World experiment. Not economic development this time—psychology. The territory of nerves and intellect. Yes, yes, but how was the City? Well, it was there. Like many newcomers to New York we had first run amok on adventures of the senses, then suddenly awoke one day to realize that the Statue of Liberty was yet to recognize our presence. Eventually we exhausted ourselves trying to catch her eye. We got pushed farther and farther back from her orbit and became depressed. Depression into further frantic adventures, into a bleeding of the spirit. Jazz could not counterbalance our depression, and we knew no other source of strength. So we left. We expect to be more at ease in California. But what about Iowa City? Do you remember the time picketing the barbershops? When one young barber pleaded, Good Christ, I don't have nothing against cutting nig, uh, Negro hair. But nobody never showed me how! Remember?

The professor and his wife remembered, but not with the same vibrations we had remembering on the road. "Times are changing fast," he said. "Picketing has already become obsolete as a method for effecting change. We've had too much of it in the past two years."

Mike, who was still holding his hat on one knee said, "Most people have never witnessed a picket line in all their lives, much less been on one."

"True, but they see them on television, and that's almost the same as being there."

"Mass culture," his wife said. "Young fellows like yourselves will have to invent something new to keep people awake, otherwise Bull Connor and Jim Clark are on their way to becoming folk heroes."

And what about Malcolm? It was on the tip of my tongue but something in the room made me not say it. "Invent something like what?" Mike asked, and I could feel him too stiffening.

"That would depend on you, wouldn't it? How much vigor and imagination you could muster."

We were silent. She lit a cigarette, and shook her bosom putting out the match. The professor rocked himself in his leather chair and kept his eyes somewhere between our heads and the ceiling. Mike, hardening by the minute, put his drink down and held his hat between his knees. Something Malcolm had said kept ringing in my head and I knew it was a mistake for us to be sitting there. How much longer would we choose to rhapsodize white folks (and many of our own too)? What held us back?

"Tell them what you've been doing, Cass," she said.

"What?" he asked.

"Oh don't be modest. They're going to find out anyhow."

"Do you mean . . . ?"

"Oh shit! He's made one of his students pregnant," she said to us. Mike fondled his hat attentively.

"Well that's no worse than you going off for a week with your acid-head lover . . . what's his name . . ." he said. I had one last toothpick left in my pocket. You know how I carry them all the time. They are cheaper than gum, and a whole lot cleaner too, I believe. So I pulled out my last toothpick and rolled it around between my lips.

"You wouldn't make an accusation like that in front of my lawyer, would you?" she said. I noticed again the bunched strength in Mike's shoulders, and running across my mind came an incident from earlier in the day when on one of those narrow Indiana highways I took a chance overtaking a truck and ended having to cut in sharply in front of it. This made the driver furious, I could see in my rear-view mirror, and he followed our bumper all the way after that until we stopped for gas. He whipped his rig into the service station too, pulled up on our passenger side, and started out towards our car with his red forearms ready, his little bead eyes sunken in and as vicious looking as a taunted boar's. Then Mike unfolded out his door—six-foot-seven, two hundred and seventy, hard—you remember how he looked in those days. The truck driver immediately found something along his dash to divert his eyes and keep him from getting out of the cab completely. We gassed up and left.

What was it holding us back? Did I see the professor's wife also with her eyes upon Mike's shoulders? "You wouldn't, would you?" she repeated.

"Why don't you let sleeping dogs lie?" he replied.

"This is no sleeping dog." And to us, "Cass had very high motives. He understands we have to get past dealing with each other as strictly political beings—I am with you on that darling—and he tried, but his approach failed. The girl refuses to have an abortion."

"Bonnie has this whole thing all wrong," he explained. "It is not half as serious as she's trying to make it."

"I don't see how anything could be more serious for you than your getting a black girl pregnant and her refusing to abort. We are not in the days of free concubinages, you know. What're you going to do when the bastard gets here?"

"Take it as a blessing. And don't pretend you are not responsible for any of this . . ."

It was past time for us to go. Who was the black girl? Was she really pregnant? How was she holding up under the whole affair? Mike laughed suddenly. "What are you two trying to do?" he said.

"Next thing I hear, you'll be drawing on each other."

"No, no. It'll never come to that," the wife said.

"It'll never come to that," the professor echoed.

What was it holding them back?

Before we left the professor and his wife, she had a request. She had for a long time wanted to do in picture journalism the story of her family in Iowa. The great-grandfather had settled there in the early nineteenth century and built a house near the river. He was a hard-working, God-fearing man who believed in freedom for all mankind, and as a follower of the abolition movement had let his place be used for one of the Underground Railroad stations. Wouldn't it be marvelous to recapture those days? There were a number of places which were used as stations still standing along the river on into Missouri, but she wanted to start with her great-grandfather's. Wouldn't it be instructive? The house was still intact, unremodeled from those old times; even the little slip at which boats used to tie up was still there. A highway ran in front the house now, but the woods behind and to the sides were virgin. Excellent for a picture essay. There was one thing missing—no more runaway slaves. Now, if she could get someone to pose for her . . . And she would pay . . .

In the end I agreed. Out of curiosity I say, but there could have been other reasons. For one, Mike and I were short on money and I thought this would be an all right way to pick up a little. But even so, there could have been other reasons.

On the following morning I met her at the house. It was an old, decayed, colonial mansion type structure, apparently abandoned long ago, with all the windows gone, and huge mounds of mold in the corners both upstairs and down. She took me to the basement to see the "station" where in-transit slaves used to be hidden. The only entrance was through a trap door in what might have been the scullery, and down a narrow ladder which her great-grandfather, or his servants, used to withdraw once the runaways were stowed. The "station" itself was a six-by-six-foot cell with a dirt floor, and walls mossy with the moisture from subterranean leaks. A little light came in from a narrow porthole at ground level with rusty iron bars over it. There were hollowed-out dirt enclaves along two walls, and a rotten table and chair. The cell was barely big enough for two, and as we turned around in it we kept bumping each other. She had brought along some of her husband's gardening clothes and a tattered straw hat which she asked me to put on. I would not change, but pulled the dirty pants and jacket over my own clothes, and put the straw hat on my head. She wanted me to pose at the rotten table looking relieved but pensive, and a little frightened if I could manage it. Difficult to explain how I felt. Being in that underground room with her was not half as easy as I had thought it would be. There was nothing nonchalant about it.

I sat at the table and I don't know what my face did, but I felt like I imagine a young girl must, the first time she prostitutes herself. The professor's wife took pictures. I stood looking through the rusty iron bars, and she snapped some more. I have never been undressed in public, nor whipped for the pleasure of others, but I believe I understand fully after those moments in Bonnie's dungeon how it must feel to be naked in the presence of strange eyes and hands that know better than anything else how to hurt you.

She took several photographs. And when we went back upstairs she took some more photographs. I couldn't tell what was happening to my face because it had lost all feeling. We went outside and she asked first would I bend over as though running through the woods away from the river. Then as though I were running towards the house behind her. Crouched, with my gut experiencing a wild pain, I spun to face the house, and in that moment saw the husband, Cass, half-hidden in an upstairs window, looking down on us with a camera up to his eye.

Later, when the moment came for me to be paid she said, "What was it we agreed on?"

I couldn't answer.

Her husband came down from his hiding place. "Do you remember what we agreed on?" she turned to him.

"Fifty cents a frame, wasn't it?" he replied, keeping a distance and with an alertness I had never noted before in his eye.

I finished removing the sweaty clothes.

"Fifty cents," she repeated, then began to compute.

I started out of the building.

She looked up as I moved, and edged closer to her husband. "Is that alright with you?" she asked. "Fifty cents? I could raise it to seventy-five."

I continued on out of the building, and the last I saw of them they stood with interlocking arms sending stony looks behind me.

At times since, I have thought myself a fool for not taking their money.

When later I found Mike at his friend's house and we were ready to leave town he asked, "Did they pay you?"

"Didn't take their money," I said.

"Why not?" I didn't answer. "That's okay," he said, "we have enough bread to get us to California." I couldn't answer Mike that morning, no more than I could now if the question were once again put. Perhaps, if you go through with your plan to become a prostitute, you will soon experience the state I was in.

Let me say, though, that if you intend to be a successful prostitute don't do as I did. Demand always ten times whatever you believe yourself to be actually worth, and payment beforehand. I hope you will see from my story why I offer such advice.

About my own situation here at present there is little new to tell. I am still waiting for God to appear in California, but my mind refuses to be a file cabinet of liturgies or a nurse-guardian to so-called heaven-producing ideologies. My mind is very absorbed in its own will to destroy and reconceive, and who knows, this might be the viable approach to God-like behavior. Help the dying die—without pain if you can—acknowledge that innocence and purity belong to the newborn.

Yet, with all this, I long for old places and familiar even if not friendly faces. Don't be surprised if you hear before long that I'm gone once again to Iowa.

Stay well love

The Pre-Jail Party

Miss Satin Bellamy—not Washington, nor Davis, nor Jefferson. There is much in a name, everybody ought to remember—Fundi, so cute, him with his sweet little self saying Bellamy? That must come from Belle Amie—you know what that means in French? As if she had ever had time for any lessons in French. Shoo! She could have taught the French one or two things would put all that stuff they got famous for to shame. So cute, he with his little self—she would have to stop calling him little seeing as how he wasn't, and that was only a way of being affectionate which he didn't always appreciate—writing to her from all over the country. Miss Satin Bellamy took one last turn in front the mirror satisfied, even though her mind was elsewhere, that the minidress indeed deserved to clothe her trim shoulders and bust, that it was doing all right the way it flared just enough from her waist down over her hips. More than six times already she had worn it, and still it made her feel new. She was very pleased with the way she looked altogether. She patted her hair over the sides, then lifted the Afro natural once again as high as it would go, then patted it down to the right level where it would assert itself without obscuring too much the ears she was about to hang with emerald green earrings. Miss Satin felt lovely. There was one flaw; at the back of her left knee a vein had begun to thicken, and she would have to move against it soon. But the rest of her smooth brown legs all up to the hemline was enough, plenty, for the time being, to keep eyes off the cording vein. Perhaps soon she would have to begin wearing darker stockings. This evening her eyes rested, without an aching muscle in her back or arm, Miss Satin Bellamy felt lovely discovering all over again how vibrant she looked in red, with the green earrings in gold settings brushing beneath her black hair. She was lovely. Were Fundi here he would have said so, and gone out to buy her flowers. So cute! But she must remember not to call him that when next they were together.

Perfumed, well-groomed, she at seven-thirty sashayed out into the warm twilight that said with its cloudless indigo sky, summer's almost here. And the pale street lights fractured by playful new leaves; with in the air a freshness she remembered from the mountains, or ocean shore, or maybe just a country day outside Los Angeles. Sashayed on her way to Cedric's three blocks the other side of Crenshaw and she wondered wouldn't it be nice to leave the car behind and walk for a change. In the end closing the garage door on the glistening Firebird having decided to walk, and setting off feeling slightly foolish along the empty sidewalk, in a city, perhaps the only one in the world, where nobody walked unless in need. She with enough money and good feelings to fly her twice to Georgia—if she ever wanted to go there—not afraid of muggers, rapists, nor the other hungry ones who people the shadows of big cities, nevertheless feeling as though her decision not to use the car stemmed from naive bravado which might later on be punished. Until it crossed her mind that this was Monday, and the shopping center through which she must pass would be bright and crowded with evening shoppers enough to make it worth the time she had spent grooming into her red dress and shoes; the looks, of course, and a whistle or two—maybe catching some man who would offer to walk her the rest of the way to Cedric's. That was the trouble with motor cars—they didn't let others see enough of what you had. Satisfied she had a pretty plenty even though in the dream it had all melted away—but that was only a dream and the real her was alive, full, warm in a red dress properly revealing beneath her black suede coat.

At the intersection where her street met Crenshaw she remembered she had not checked the mailbox. The special delivery letter, which must have been the postman ringing her door four-thirty in the afternoon, left stuck in the screen had made her forget. Air mail, special delivery. Only Fundi. No one else sent special delivery to her address; and she knew it even before recognizing the handwriting, in a way to make her wonder had she been wishing to hear from him. Pleased, was she? More than that. But not happy quite. In her coat pocket she carried the letter still unopened, and realizing how it had made her forget to check for any other mail the feeling came back of a slight omen why she hadn't opened the letter as usual, right away, but walked off feeling not as though life were threatened, but that the next few days, or weeks, or years were destined to be immeasurably unhappy, with a fresh kind of suffering she would have to face in all its power and uncertainty. An omen. But everyone knew bad dreams meant good events in life. So thinking to herself, and shaking off the will to back up, relent, and read Fundi's special delivery letter, check the mailbox, then drive herself over to Cedric's; refusing to let an omen determine the style of her legs or their direction.

The shops as she expected were brightly lit, their windows gay with spring fashions and accessories, the glittering glass in places casting back her reflection chic as the most sophisticated mannequin, except she was for real, and soft—where she wanted to be— when she wanted to be. Tonight she wanted to be. And for a moment thought there must be something wrong with her like old age, which couldn't be true because at thirty she knew certainly the difference between sentimentalism and for-realness, and it wasn't the first that impelled her through the doors of May Co., into their shoe shop and wandering beyond it. Content with the impulse to buy Fannie Mae something. It wasn't the first. The realization driving contentment deeper, so that she felt it all the way from her throat to her navel, and heard only from a distance the young man saying "Good God! Baby, you got to let me do something for you" in a deep sweetened voice as she brushed past him dressed pink and brown like the latest Esquire model, complete with breast-pocket kerchief, honey-brown face smooth and serious except for the lips quivering nervous and uncertain. Fundi never wore complete outfits. Fundi was dark black. Fundi was . . . even though the comparison was of no importance. She wanted perfume. Fannie Mae would dig on something wild smelling. The wigs were pretty too—expecially one cut as an Afro-blond that would go great with the black ensembles Fannie liked to

wear. Ha! As if Fannie Mae was going to be wearing any kind of ensembles where she was going. What the hell kind of clothes did
women wear in prison? After all her friends who had been there she
didn't even know that. Didn't even know if they could wear perfume
or silken bras or their own panties. Way they did people, woman
probably couldn't wear nothing but cotton bloomers and blue jean
shirts, and they probably cut off all your hair too. She hoped Fannie
Mae was ready for the worst. But Fannie Mae had heart. Thinking
back to the time when they were both picked up on Western Avenue,
and the two cracker police instead of driving them to the station
pulling up in the dark beside some cemetery and telling them to take
off their drawers. She wasn't wearing any nohow, but when Fannie
Mae told them to kiss her ass she felt frightened and wished she did
have something to pull off and show them she wasn't not complying.
The crackers were too big, mad-dog looking in their eyes, and she
had heard too terrible stories of what they could do with nightsticks.
She knew what they could do with their guns, and wasn't nothing she
could do against them. She, nor Fannie Mae, nor the bad talk pimp
who was supposed to be around to save them from situations just
like this. She would have gladly pulled off something, especially
when the two police got out and dragged her from the back seat
cage, the taller one just a broad animal something in the night shoving her into the front seat saying "You don't see you don't hear you
don't talk, and you could run if you want. I would like that." Fingering his gun. Then joining the other in the cage with Fannie Mae. She
was afraid to look. She was ashamed to look. While Fannie Mae
fought the two beasts who it later came were just teasing. She was
afraid to look and so enraged she cursed Fannie Mae herself for
starting trouble, until they got serious, and the rubber licks came
fast and hard as if between her own legs and upside her own head
and Fannie Mae wouldn't scream but moaned and kept cursing,
even after they were through and laughingly straightened their uni-
forms while the second one said "That'll keep you for a while. And
you tell all your black whore friends they better go back to Georgia.
We don't want them polluting Los Angeles." Soon after dumping
Fannie on the ground, and shoving her out in the cool night air, dis-
appearing in their near-silent official car, without lights, as effective-

ly as phantoms, brothered by that shuffling out of nowhere in the shape of the black pimp, nigger-brown pimp, with honey-sweet voice asking "Y'all okay?" Fannie Mae bled but never stopped cursing all the way to the hospital, where they reported an attempted rape by assailants unknown before they could see the doctor. And Fannie Mae refused to stay for observation, refused any but the most immediate medication, even though it took five weeks in bed before she could show her face on the avenue again. That all was a long ways in the past. Yet here Fannie was, ready to go up again, and this time nobody knew if the judge wasn't going to say years instead of months, but Fannie Mae had heart. And she, Miss Satin Bellamy, on the first floor in May Co., unangered, searching out a gift, which wasn't to belatedly apologize to Fannie but give her as best as possible some piece of this new feeling that came from where she did not know but needed sharing. A wig would, as a matter of fact, not do. As a matter of fact she would remember when she saw Fannie Mae to tell her give up those damn wigs anyhow. Could that be Fundi? Could it be him and his talk about harmony of self? Satin moved on from the wig counter. Perfume? Shoes? Books? Cosmetics? Clocks? Clocks. Recalling bygone childhood days seen dimly, in which a brown wood clock hung dead silent on the wall until someone tugged the chain to make it go tick tock for three or four seconds. A brown wood clock with yellow numbers and green hands without any life of their own exposed to the dust on her fingers when no one was looking, making no resistance except to cring once each time the short hand passed twelve. An inconsequential thing in an inconsequential childhood, somehow as memory so important she could want to re-create it again, and pass it on. Would Fannie Mae appreciate a brown clock? Knowing all the time that what Fannie Mae stood ready to appreciate was not so important as what she needed to appreciate. Looking up to encounter once again the breathing Esquire full-page model, only the colors were different on him this time, his skin dark-black like Fundi's, and his face quite calm but firm, very likeable. "Could I help you?" he asked in such a complete voice she wanted immediately to say yes in many ways but controlled herself to reply "You got any brown clocks that hang up on the wall?" "Brown clocks that hang up on the wall?" "Yes." "Is this for your own home

or a gift?" "A gift." "We have some very nice ones—for the den or
kitchen or living room," he said, unlocking a vertical cabinet of high
polished glass, and stepping aside for her to see. Such fine-looking
clocks! Brass, gold, silver, and shimmering glass. Square, round,
diamond. Such fine styles in the numbers! On one in particular, diamond shaped with the numbers resting on a circle, the Roman lines
so bold, vigorous, yet contained so they didn't crowd each other.
Clear and powerful to the eye, but never overflowing the boundaries
of their shapes. Such elegance! In gold, with a brilliant chain suspended by a hold the size of a cigar, itself ringed in a way that reminded her of the fine tools at an apartment where she had spent a
night once. Wouldn't Fannie Mae trip out on such a clock? "How
much is that one?" she asked, pointing. The salesman followed her
finger and answered, "Fifty-nine ninety-nine. Best buy in the house
at that price." He took it down and brought it to the counter. He dis-
assembled the case so she could see the works, but she found his
brown fingers instead and was pleased to let them take her attention.
Dark black. Brown. What would they do mixed with hers? ". . .
Swiss made," he was saying. "Guaranteed for life. You have a very
good buy here." "It's nice. The only thing, though, I wanted a brown
one. You don't have any brown ones?" He turned away to look
through his other cases, and she imagining his full back in her hands
had to laugh at herself. Smile at the elementary pleasure she felt,
quite disconnected from him as a potential investment of time and
energy. Wouldn't it be a pleasure with such a man to walk beside?
He didn't have any brown clocks. "That's all right," she said, "I'll
take this one." Hadn't he smelled her perfume? Hadn't he seen how
fine she was and styled? "Are you in charge of this department?"
she asked. "No. I'm just starting here." "Really? What makes a fine
man like you want to be selling clocks?" He continued busily writing
up the sales ticket and didn't answer. Until, "I like clocks. You must
too to buy one like this for a gift." "Not so much as I like my friend,"
she said, feeling as powerful and complete as a Roman numeral.
"Your friend is very lucky," he said. "I like you too," she couldn't
help saying, uncertain if she had truly said what she meant. Yet he
smiled. "I should really never have let you say it first. I like you."
She paid him, took the gift and left.

On through the shopping center, past the grocery store and drug stores and baby shop: she who had never had a baby except once, and then in a way not pleasant to recall. She had never even seen it, just felt the man's fat fingers poking things around inside her, with her back against the cold table and nothing to see but his fat unhealthy face and discolored eyes, in the dim light of an upstairs loft dark at the corners, and for moments at a time a strange feeling that the shadows were full of eyes with their whites hidden, but that was only her Southern upbringing with its stock of ghosts and phantoms and other superhuman beings. Nothing to see but the unshaven jowls of this strangely disconnected man poking around inside her without passion, little beads of perspiration hung on his forehead and upper lip but never dropping. The cold table, the dim room, and she never even seeing what it was he took from her but dying, so it seemed, when the pain came, when that moment which her body knew without mind was a moment of eternal severance, dying with nothing to see but that momentary look of fright upon the man's face so he kept his eyes between her legs and warned her to be still. Dead still. No, it was not pleasant to recall. That day in her life which before it she believed would set her free, that hour which in fact marked the beginnings of darkest imprisonment, darker than anything the sheriff or police could conjure. Imprisoned in a state of barrenness. Two sides. Twin sides. The freedom she had in her young days craved, and with it the death of her womb, the end to all prospects for bringing new light into the universe. Pleasure and freedom forever transient, and it was only much later she discovered there was another pleasure, freedom, freedom, that went on and on, before her, around and beyond her, and she having forfeited practically all her given privilege to be a part of it. Not pleasant at all, but at least tonight Miss Satin Bellamy recalled in fleeting moments the horror of that condition without tears. She neither cried nor lamented internally, she who having forfeited her finest function in the union had never had, would never have a baby. Involuntarily she smiled at the sales clerk behind the glass window of the stork shop and passed on. To cross in front the ice cream and hair-dressing parlors, and into the wide uphill parking lot dense with cars of every shape. There was a true freedom. Walking. With the texture of the asphalt reaching all the way to her hips. But the clock grew heavy, and before she turned up Buckingham Road she sat down on a bus stop bench to rest for a few minutes.

Fundi at the back of her mind, Fundi at the front of her mind, Fundi inside her pocket in a letter she postponed opening. Coming out in the people she saw. Fundi. Somewhere between St. Louis and somewhere east, because even though he didn't in his last letter say in which direction he was running she knew it was away from her and that would mean east, pointed at the Atlantic. Yet the Atlantic was the western ocean, wasn't it? Eastern too, depending if you were sitting on a bus stop bench in Los Angeles, California, U.S.A. A useless brain game, having nothing to do with Fundi being so far away from her when tonight she would have him walk beside her in peace. Or sit beside her, hold her hand. Satin tried, in surprise of herself, for the moment outside of herself, tried reaching through mind and feeling to wherever Fundi might be. Tried reaching through image of mind and will, demanding it be revealed wherever he was she wanted to be with him now, and for a short second when there was contact in her vision she felt profoundly complete. And free too to pull the letter from her pocket. Postmark Kingston, New York.

Dear Satin,

It is disheartening. Here I am, survivor of numerous storms, about to complete my thirty-fifth winter, and still am able to say so very little to the beauty of rain. I sit here, watch, and realize it has always been a significant force in me, and if I were asked to narrate the most touching moments in my life I would find rain at the center of each. Rain in all its shapes and intensities. And, as I have lately discovered, its colors. That's what would be at the core of it all, that sky-drip, water-drip, moistening me from the sky, uniformly remote, yet everlastingly intimate in its myriad methods of penetrating the soul . . .

She stopped reading. Always taking too long to say what he wanted to say. Fundi's letters were too demanding. They wanted too much time, always, and she wasn't in the mood for playing profound. Nor for pretty poetry words. Secure as she was in the awareness of her own substance, and that of which it was a small part, such words seemed trifling. She would finish his letter another time, not let it muddy up the pleasure she felt in wanting to be with him, the swift sweet sensations when she imagined what it would be like were they really together in this minute. She put Fundi's letter back into her pocket, and continued on her way to Cedric's.

"Whatcha got under your arm, girl?"

"What it look like?"

"Champagne."

"You're out of your mind if you expect me to be bringing champagne for a set of whores and pimps to drink." She didn't want to be talking like that.

"Whores and pimps be the best kind of people, girl. We doctor up all the suffering in the world, you know that. You one the best doctoresses yourself. But what you got?"

"Lemme in the damn door then maybe you could find out."

Still grinning Cedric slipped back and drew the door wide. If she were a bulldozer she would have walked right over him, rolled him to pulp; but she didn't know why. Maybe his hair—that goddamned hog-greased pompadour standing four inches above his forehead like he was a junior Kirk Douglas or something. Or the paisley vest; or the half-dollar-size cuff links; or the red skinny pants tight up into his crotch; or just his plain black silly face grinning like it knew the secrets of the whole world. Whatever it was the anger churned inside her, and she was sincere in the slap up side his head when he stroked her ass.

"Good God woman! What you eating these days?" Cedric said, laughing it off. "Independent whores must be doing real well for you to be slapping me like that. But don't do it no more, hear?" Still laughing, but she knew he was serious. Maybe that was it, after all, the violence alert and desperate right beneath his skin. In bed or with other weapons. That swift wiping out that was a mighty madness. It was a mistake for her to come. Yet there was Fannie Mae coming out of the corner towards her smiling, with arms open, Fannie Mae who had told her what, and showed her how to do so many times, like a big sister; who was in fact a true sister, so her bosom said as they embraced, and Satin forgetting Cedric found herself wanting to cry. "Times agreeing with you girl. You sure look good," said Fannie Mae, holding her at shoulder length. "You ain't directly headed for the old folk's home neither," Satin replied, forcing her eyes to remain dry. "Who all your company?" Besides Cedric and two other women whom Satin knew there was Cedric's buddy JoJo and two strange men whom she had never seen. "They friends of mine from San Francisco," Fannie Mae said. "Let me introduce you . . . But what you got? Didn't I hear you tell Cedric you got something for me?"

Without saying a word Satin walked to the table. She opened the package and held up the clock for Fannie Mae to see the diamond-shaped face, the perfect Roman numerals. Not a brown clock like the one of her childhood, but perfect in itself, she knew, without being an engineer. "I wanted to get you a brown one," she said, but stopped when they all broke out laughing. She had never thought about how the clock would strike them.

"You can count the hours one by one," Cedric said to Fannie Mae. "It got a calendar too?"

Fannie Mae laughed herself, saying, "Goddamn, Satin! You want me to know I'm serving time, don't you."

One of the other whores chimed, "It's pretty, but they ain't going to let you keep it. They got their own clocks in jail."

"That's right," said one of the strange men. "They got their own clocks and you never see them. All you get is a bell. A bell telling you time to get up; time to bathe; time to eat; time to go to sleep. Pretty clock ain't no use to nobody in jail."

"How much you pay for it?" Fannie Mae asked. But Satin couldn't find a voice to answer . . . She wasn't confused. She was angry. And did not like the feeling descending ever since Cedric's touch, coming down strong now, warning she was about to lose her mind and do something she didn't know what. "Sixty dollars for a clock! For me?" Then she began to laugh and cry, and tried to embrace Satin again but Satin pushed her away.

"Go on bitch. Like they say, it ain't goin do you no good in jail nohow."

"Sixty dollars! It more than anything I make in such a long time I can't help crying."

Times had changed. Fannie's cheeks had grown round and puffy. Girdles no longer hid the soft rolls around her hips and stomach. Wasn't that why she was going to jail? Couldn't no longer sit at the Black Fox bar crossing her legs that way to get all the customers she wanted. Even on the street corner she didn't do nothing but pick up a cop. And what's going to happen when Satin gets to that? Vowing she never would grow fat and ugly, "Much money as you made all over L.A. you crying about sixty dollars?"

"Don't pay her no attention," Cedric said. "I take good care of her."

"I ain't complaining," Fannie Mae said, "but it'd be nice to be making my own money like I'm used to."

"You just sad cause you going to jail," Cedric said. "That's all. Why don't we stop this fooling around and really have a party, eh?"

"Right," said the second strange man. "I don't drink but I got something here ready to send everybody to cloud nine. Let's go."

Wasn't she angry? It was worse than that. Where she had to destroy somebody, it didn't matter who. She looked around the room, and the afternoon state of her body and mind was a distant dream where some angel or devil had told her she was peaceful. A distant dream, trite, quite false in comparison to the smell of marijuana and wine and whisky, the smell of men and female bodies letting go, getting ready to give away like sweating balloons the thing—spirit or whatever it was—they contained. She didn't like the feeling. She didn't approve the feeling in herself, nor the wreckage she knew this night would leave behind, but her legs couldn't clinch a value strong enough to take her back out into the dark night and the walk alone home to the apartment alone and bed alone. Where was the value in that? With Fundi it would be different. But alone? Who was she to presume herself against this need of her flesh to tear itself and its kind, bruise itself in the destruction of flesh that cannot be done alone? In the heavy-smelling room the feel of her nerves relaxing themselves. Untangling. Laying themselves out in orderly, if unappeased lines. Satisfaction would come later. Cedric, JoJo, the strangers were all strong men, heavily planted in this swirling universe. Was she giggling? Only at the realization of how easy it was going to be embracing one of them so she too would become heavy and like a firm place. Fannie Mae was gone. Her wig taken off, her shoes; herself at ease in the middle of the room doing the dog. Music coming up. As if supplanting the atmosphere, so it had no beginning, just a sweet weight that let you know it was your breath going down to wherever breath goes, spreading out from there to head, arms, and toes. Give me more. Music. Vibrating one past idleness or thought, all obstacles between me and the underworld, aboveworld, past-future world where nobody was afraid of being common. Her short skirt lapping against her thighs; arms, head, and body making a sweet breeze for her nostrils. Satin danced. The men came one by one showing her their shoulders, and their arms. She smiled, waiting. They passed on one by one. "What you talking about!" Fannie Mae exclaimed. "Play James Brown again. I feel good." The men came one by one, and it was no less than she expected to have happen when she found herself close in somebody's arms, with his breath like heavy steam coming down her face. No less than she needed, perhaps desired. She wasn't sure about that last. Doubts came back again, and although the dance still had her she wanted to sit down and straighten things out in her mind. He lit another joint, but she passed. Nor wine nor whisky either. Nor gin sweet-smelling like a big heavy flower. Where was she? "You like it?" She could hear Fannie Mae's voice. And a man's replying, "What you saying honey!" Fannie's going to work herself to death. What? Wouldn't he be laughing still, maybe behind her back, when it was all over? And she Satin, what was she doing with another strange hand passing upon her body here and there, seeking her legs, measuring for the right moment. Where was she going? Coming down from? She let the fingers touch her pants. Then moved them firmly away. What for? Where was she going? Why wasn't Fundi here? The hand coming again warm and rough grating along her nylons. Be so nice if it were Fundi's. She would know the meaning of the game then. Could there be a meaning here she missed? Seeking this stranger's eyes all lost in her direction but not seeing her she could tell. Letting him stroke her twice before taking hold of the hand again, only this time a brief lingering before moving it away. Why wasn't Fundi here? He could save everything by making it known what was going on. He would show her where she wanted to be and end this blind fumbling. She closed her eyes, no longer wanting to see this strange face relying so much on her for what she didn't have to give but eager to accept the lie she knew well how to give. Perhaps with eyes closed Fundi might come. But it was the hand again—stronger than hers this time, and what she would have had to do to get away didn't seem worth the effort. Why wasn't Fundi here? She was no stone. And exhausted with compromising. With taking the thing at hand while waiting for the best to come. It was not her fault when she opened her mouth to a kiss or her legs to strange hands. Not her fault it was so impossible not to lie while waiting for the fine best to come. She showed the stranger she had very fine breasts too, then relaxed. Where was she? Back before buying clocks in an indigo sky deep down to enfold her. Peace and pleasure. Gone by. Pleasure come back like a vibrating drum at her center, and somewhere herself saying no even while it was happening to her and promising greater still. No, saying in a voice clear as a small bell; vibrations newborn, vibrations without power that she needed on her side to stem the liquidation of her life in daze and fantasy. Wasn't the truth sweet? Wasn't the truth sweet? Such ugly sweetness. And horrifying. Like demons in the dark. A sheet of paper somebody once said; a sheet of paper which ever has two sides but always is the same. No. It would have to be NO. She could say NO the voice newborn like a young bell in need of nourishment. The sources within her come down from this state of daze and fantasy to a true midday bell, crisp, clear, resounding, pushing every demon over the edge of the universe. Truth sweet like a piece of twin-faced paper. Yes. No. No. Yes. Yes. No. Recalling the afternoon state in which she was at one and peaceful. Wishing for the smoothness of her own sheets and a state of mind without need. And Fundi somewhere in the distance like a messenger ignorant of the message it was his call to deliver, the purpose, which in a second stood clear in her and she could have told him. Fundi off in the distance chasing the very peace of which he already had so much it had become his burden. A state of mind without need. Not the fantasy of herself—an enormous hole capable of sucking in the entire universe. Even so yes-saying, feeling in disappointment the newborn NO fluttering submerged in its own weakness. Like a young bird in need of its mother's wing. And she? Yes saying against not her will but her something she that although not left behind could not overtake her. To come down in a room already dark with the man unfastening her dress and stockings; and she quite undecided what to do about him for the moment doing nothing. Uncertain whether she desired his hands or was unhappy with them she did nothing. Until he shuddered in release then said, "What's the matter with you bitch? Why don't you stop acting like a lump of white Mary and do something? What's the matter, you can't talk? Or you too good for me?" The last thing she expected. "Since when you stop knowing you're supposed to please somebody?" Slapping her hard before she could move or say anything. She flailed back, even while knowing better, hitting for his eyes and groin, with the taste of blood in her mouth, the smell of blood coming up deep down in her liver. Hitting, flailing at this estranged monster in the dark, and screaming not because of his blows. She herself at last released, set free to be as monstrous as her feelings said, become with a gigantic screaming howl a terrified monstrosity terrifying, bent on terrifying, completed in making sure every ear and mind within reach felt and suffered her without escape. And the man unheeding, insulated by his greater muscle strength, beat her head and face, the only places beside her arms he did not have covered; her arms without power to crack him into her feelingness. Blood came from drops to a trickle, promising a greater rush, and still was not enough to satisfy the dry clamouring in her mouth, her throat, the dry clamouring throughout her being urgent for the wetness, the wet thick heavy sweetness. Her arms not strong enough to crack this strange man but with power enough so it took Cedric and JoJo and the second stranger to pull them apart and release her victim. And even then not seeing the blood come in steady pulse down his neck, not noticing the look of terror captured in his eyes; noticing nothing except the sweet taste on her lips and the urgent tormenting wish for more.

When Cedric stopped the car in front of her apartment house, Satin lifted her head off Fannie Mae's shoulder, gathered up her purse and opened the door. "You all right?" Fannie Mae asked.

"Yeah, I'm all right," she said. Cedric was silent and stiff, his rigid shoulders foretelling that this was another instance of his being put upon that Fannie Mae would have to pay for. Satin stepped out into the night that was not damp, and smelled like metal dust hanging everywhere in the atmosphere.

"You take care of yourself, hear," Fannie Mae said.

"You do the same," she replied.

"And don't forget to write to me. You know how you could write them letters!"

Cedric gunned the car engine. She stood with her hand still on the door and said, "I'll write."

"And listen, girl, that's a beautiful clock. All right if I bring it around for you to keep till I come back?"

"Sure."

"Well, you take care of yourself, now."

"You do the same," Satin replied, and started for the steps into her building.

Satin's Dream

"Fundi, you have come back. You are a giant!" Exclaiming as he stood there unexpectedly in her doorway so tall and bold, his eyes shining with a power she had never seen in a black man before. But he would not speak. "I wasn't expecting you. I am not dressed. When did you get back?" Fingering the wrinkled quilt robe, then holding it tight together down the front where the buttons were broken off. "When did you get back Fundi?" And he standing in the doorway silent and shining, saying not a word, discomposing her with his steady eyes. Did the awkward feeling of her nakedness beneath the robe come from him? In a twinkle moment to feel disjointed from what she had been up to all day. "Well, aren't you going to say something?" Even as right there before her eyes he swelled more than two sizes bigger, threatened to darken the whole doorway which was the first light she had seen all day. Behind her, past the other door closed, she had been all day without any thought of Fundi, without any thought except pleasing the desires of a short-term lover, and herself too, pleasing herself too she would have to admit, even though that didn't come first because Fundi was her pleasure, was her true pleasure whom she didn't know was coming. To stand in her doorway shutting out almost all the light but saying not a word, stand there letting her know his senses penetrated the walls, giving off some kind of warning, a puzzle, which she felt incapable to decipher but could not ignore. He made her feel dirty looking at her that way. Unclean. So she began to shrink and grow small to the ground, helpless to stop all her fine self from crumbling down, her fine ass, legs, titties, which had been so keenly at play a short time ago diminishing in girth and texture, leaving her skeletal like a gone consumptive growing short, getting small to the ground beneath towering Fundi, towering over her, letting by no light, not even between his legs become so thick, melded, like a single rock column. And her lips too, and cheeks, which had taken hundreds of kisses and returned in the past few hours alone being wrinkled, dried down, until Fundi said, "The road came to an end, and I had to come back so I could get started again."

"I am glad to see you. Stay and talk to me for a while." But her voice had shrunk too small and couldn't reach him.

"You are still engaged in your punishment," he said. "That gets me started all right. In a minute I'll begin on all the landscapes and faces still waiting on me. This time will be the last."

"I'm so glad you're back," she said, wanting for him to pull her in his arms, or just touch her. "I didn't know you were coming, but this is the best surprise."

"I have very little time" he said, "and there are several things that must be done. The road came to an end and I had to come back so I could get started again."

"I would have combed my hair and put on a new dress, and cleaned the house, and you would never have caught me like this," she said, forgetting for a second and opening the robe to show part of her nakedness. "You don't have to look at me that way."

"I have just enough time left for a last journey," he said, "so I'll get started. Thanks for setting me off again. You can go back to your room now."

"Why don't you get angry with me? Get angry Fundi, and stay. Don't leave me to get any smaller."

"The road came to an end and I had to . . ."

"Fuck the road! As if the road were something alive, in need of love. This is me. I am here. Look at me, Fundi!"

". . . come back so I could get started again. Take care of yourself."

"Fundi . . ." she couldn't help screaming. And screamed again so loud her buried ancestors perked up. But he didn't hear her. In-

stead, from behind the closed door came the temporary lover, naked
as a white ape, hair shaggy down his chest and thick around his legs,
bounding like a naked animal which she didn't know what he was
going to do, still his normal size which was nowhere near as powerful
as Fundi, and she felt ashamed of his smallness and wanted to hide
him from Fundi's eyes. She didn't know what he was about to do
with such a mad look on his sharp-nose face, and shouted for him to
go back, go back, but could not stand in his way from fear of being
trampled down. She could only stand helpless as he bounded
towards the doorway naked as he had been with her these past
hours, cleaved Fundi with a leap, and disappeared into the street below, naked and silent. While Fundi immediately flowed together,
turned with neither hurry nor dispatch to take his massive self away
from her door. "Fundi!!" she screamed, but it was only a whisper, as
she saw for the first time there was no back to Fundi's body, and she
could see into him as through an open window the heart, lungs, liver,
imbedded in the hulk of his muscles, coupled by red and white ma-
chinery. Then she couldn't stop herself from flying too down the
sidewalk, the robe like a quilt cape pendant from her shoulders,
calling Fundi, whose stride kept him ever just beyond her reach, calling in a voice that was barely a whisper. Unable to turn back though
she knew he would never hear her. Until the street was no longer a
sidewalk beneath spreading shade trees but a narrow gash in the
land with steep sides and a railway coming through, and ahead
Fundi strolling the way drop-heads do on coke or some other high,
even though she could feel before seeing the massive grey train coming towards them, and called. The wind, hot and rough between her
legs, breasts spilling to the ground forcing her to step sideways
around them, she called, tripping over what she discovered in her
hands to be a real-life back complete with muscles and nerve fittings
the size of Fundi. She called, yet her voice, champion of countless
low encounters in bar and bedroom, remained too small. And her
legs without substance enough to bring her up to him, without substance to do any more than a rhythmic pounding in search of grace
when she needed above all to hurry; rhythm without grace, an invisible net restraining her from reaching to warn Fundi, the train
coming full in sight now making very little noise, but driving waves

of hot air like invisible buffets that displaced her breath with pain. They were suddenly in a dim tunnel steep, smooth, without escape. If only she could warn Fundi, together they would not die, could not die, under the wheels of this menacing iron worm; and Fundi, what the hell was he doing? Begging for it? Strolling like a blind man down the middle of the tracks without hearing back, and her voice unable to reach him, her legs refusing to take her so she could snap his back in place. Goddamn, she loved that man. She who had never loved anyone, not even herself before, the feeling welled up in a last frantic scream, "FUNDI!!"

It was the doorbell jarring Satin awake, and at first, confused from the dream, she jumped naked from her bed and started to answer but soon recovered and checked herself. She was expecting no one. She could tell from around the drawn shades the sun was still up outside. The clock said four-thirty. Miss Satin Bellamy was interested in seeing no one today before seven, and whoever was at her door could kiss her lovely ass for interrupting her sleep.

She sat on the bed before her mirror and lit a cigarette. Admiring her tits she recalled the dream. Was it an omen? She tried not to think, and jokingly cursed at her Southern country upbringing. Was it an omen? She couldn't help standing up full in front the mirror, and letting herself feel relieved at seeing she was all there. The loss of limb and curve had been so real in the dream. But in fact nothing had shrunk or disappeared. Miss Satin Bellamy was all here, and whoever was ringing her doorbell in the middle of the afternoon could stand there until they got tired and went home. Who was that hairy man in the dream? She lay back down. And Fundi? Coming back to her house so big and splendid! But it was only a dream. If she could have seen into him that way in real life she would have known better than to send him away. What's done is done. She could love him all she wanted in her dreams, but in real life she knew which end was up. Yet, could it be him out there come as a surprise to her door? Her stomach made butterflies. And she would have left the bed again, except reason told her wasn't no way he could have driven from Iowa to Los Angeles overnight. Just yesterday she had had a letter saying where he was.

Satin lay back in the bed and spread her legs beneath the covers.

It felt good being in bed by herself. She didn't feel sleepy, or even lazy. Today for the first in a long time she felt rested, a new vigor running through her veins. And maybe, just maybe, coming home by herself last night might be the cause, although she couldn't really believe so. How can there be relaxation or any of the things that bring comfort where there is no man? Whatever could take the place of man, that only power she knew which breached the tension of her womb and set her free as a molten kitten? There was something new today. The tension was not absent, but it did not interfere with her lying between silk sheets admiring her room which on Fundi's suggestion before he left she had painted rose and decorated with pink curtains. And a pink rug paid for by her own fine tail. Fundi always had a lot of words and suggestions but not much else. Today, at peace, unashamed, alone in her bed, Satin took pleasure in recounting the many good things her body had charmed her way, including Fundi. Where would I be without it? she thought, moving her hips between the covers. A fair living, and bewitching someone like Fundi too. Then laughed at the though that after all, could be, she was the one bewitched.

Julia

WORD FREE, SPIRIT FREE
SPIRIT FREE, WORD FREE
WORD FREE, SPIRIT FREE, WORD
FREE, WORD FREE, SPIRIT FREE SPIRIT
FREE, SPIRIT FREE, FREE,
FREE, FREE, FREEDOM!
WORD FREE, SPIRIT FREEDOM, FREEDOM
FREEDOM, FREEDOM, NOW!
FREEDOM NOW!

The songs were all about freedom of the spirit, of the soul—in spite
of cracked skulls, smashed arm bones, broken ribs—and her sitting
there alone in the middle of all these faces with no one to touch, feeling against all world like Jael the wife of Heber armed hammer
and spike, but without a victim. When would she forget the Bible?
The Bible. And the young men singing on the stage, the *Snick Freedom Singers*, they too had been nurtured on the Bible she could tell
("... home to my grave and be free") not only because of their songs
but also by their display of that aggressive timidity so proper when
one has been conditioned to the constant surveillance of a tough
God. When would she forget the Bible? Cousin Ollie dead and gone
surviving in the word, coming even without being summoned, the
word insisted upon as sure-up against the wickednesses of this
world. And all the serious faces. The tight white faces gleaming in
the lowered auditorium light, neither hostile nor in love, and certainly not puzzled, because—she had learned some years ago—they

never puzzled over the things that made them comfortable. And having not moved on the singers they must in their seats be quite at ease and this made her resentful. In her own hard-backed chair hostile, resentful as a hen over new chickens, a murderess in heat driving spike after spike through the insensate faces, until it occurred, what did she want anyway? And she felt ashamed of herself at the answer, dirty, as though a debased side of her nature which in one aspect of mind she knew to be nonexistent had indeed undermined its way into herself, and she knowingly had let it. Even though she had recognized the signs all day while giving her imagination the nameless zippered crotches along Main Street, and, further, stretching, embellishing each detail in the unfastening, loosening, and her fingers slipping in between the rough cloth to a delicious sensation. It had been nothing shameful then. Along the bright cold sidewalk of Main Street, a contradiction she had yet to feelingly resolve, this mixture of clean sunshine and chilling wind, it had seemed normal enough to imagine herself on her way to or perhaps already within a warm room, not alone, but a man there in rough cloth, a strong-muscled man like General whom they had goddamn them taken away. Like General, who would not again come before her eyes for so many months, whom she might oh God let it not be true never again see, or taste, or hear. With her need, her yearning come down upon her on the sidewalk, oh let it be, she in a warm room against the rough cloth of a man. In her imagination choosing this one, that one, another, many in quick succession, whose faces she would not see, whose voices she would not hear held hard against the rough cloth of a chest or shoulder. It had seemed normal then—not normal, comforting—walking down Main Street in her imagination satisfied, and somehow no offense given to General.

No more.

Tonight, sitting among all these white faces. Longing for General who sang so well. Were it he up on the stage, with a warm room not too far along in the night for them alone! General! Not there, and her feeling dirty, ashamed of her longing, the imagining that converted the *Snick* boys into his shape, his power, and all these white faces seeing, having equal claim as she into antagonists, the enemy, capable, quite ready to shut her out, though the staged pain was hers, and she without all the ways open to them of addressing heart-aches. She couldn't fly to Bermuda for the holidays. In her heart a murderous hammer and spike, cracking skulls, pinning the bloody heads to whatever, just so the blood ran out, ran free, and disappeared into the solid earth where all things were equal. She did not want to die: it was offensive to want to kill. Offensive against Cousin Ollie to whom she owed her bringing up, and herself too who had never quite stopped believing in the word—THOU SHALT NOT KILL. Oh General! And the white girl sitting beside her patting a foot to the singing—white bitch, I know your wants—patting her foot with glazed eyes behind spectacles to a song of pain that wasn't hers but which she could preempt at a moment's notice and get away with. Damn! Why did being a woman have to be so confusing? Marcia, a decent girl, with neither pride nor obtuseness. And the white faces around, no Bull Connors here, no Jim Clarks. Confusing. Because Julia knew what she felt was right and she knew it was also wrong, and, when she was honest, what pleased her most was what shamed her too. So continue to sit there and feel the singing tug at her insides. Resisting it. This thing that belonged to her but which these white faces and Marcia had all assumed by proxy. Belonged to her, though she could not fully take it or make it fully into what she desired. She could cry. Sitting there in this sea of white faces, frail, black, slender, choked up on her own longing, the multiple need for vengeance and comfort, and no end in sight. She could cry. It would be such a release to cry the way General could let her against his shoulder, and no one here, no one but the four singing black faces on stage, the shapeless people and Marcia, no one to touch at a time when she longed from so deep within her to be touched. The singing continued and they clapped hands. The auditorium clapped hands and swayed in its seat. And she could keep from crying—if only General were here—she must keep from crying, she would, though she would neither clap nor pat her feet nor sway, and pray God not a single one of them touched her because then . . . FREEDOM! FREEDOM! FREEDOM! . . . Uhuru they say in Africa. Thank God for the Mau Mau, warriors, giant conquerors up from the earth, their women, slender, black, tense, constant at their sides, women of warriors, woman of warriors satisfied all treaties were a long ways

off, the battle just begun. Please let not a single one touch her, neither in their kind of friendliness nor any other way, mau mau uprisen in her veins. Her elation somebody else's death and vice versa.
That was true. Three stitched-up scalps, two broken arms, a
patched-up face among the four boys singing, singing of a fifth not
there, last seen retrieved from a muddy backwoods stream with near
every bone in his body broken. For whom death must have been
quite a joy to his conquerors. In spite of the word. THOU SHALT
NOT KILL. Julia, breasts tender and pained with longing for a hard
man, iron-loined herself, tonight would have no trouble at all finish-
ing them off one by one, pulping blood and white matter out of their
brains, so they would know, know anguish, believe anguish, her anguish. She refused to stand when they started "We Shall Over-
come."

Bloodstones

Julia took a last turn before her mirror and was very satisfied with the way she looked. She was pleased that the dress still fit so well, since it had taken her a long time to get up the nerve to buy one like it. By the standards of her class it was too long and shapeless. The girls back in Louisiana would have laughed at her for appearing so "African." But she liked the way the dress made her feel as she turned . . . regal . . . not hugging too close; yet attendant in places where it pleased her to show. She selected emerald green stones for her ears, and felt lovely discovering over again how vibrant she looked in the flowing red dress. A touch of the Diorissimo which General had sent for the inside of her arms. She was pleased with her arms . . . smooth, sweet honey-brown arms. She hoped they never got to be as sinewy as Lily's. She was pleased with herself from top to toe. A little current, that would jump out and make her vibrate all over if it so happened she came to be touched. She did not let her thoughts dwell on that.

Perfumed, well-groomed, Julia stepped out while the sun was in its last hour. She closed her apartment door and started down the long veranda to the steps. As she passed Lily's door it opened, and the white girl said, "Well, looka here! Don't tell me somebody's finally in for a good time this evening. Wow! That outfit is a smasher."

She was in her black and pink negligee as usual, with her hair in rollers. The skin around the outside of her thighs and in between her breasts was just one step away from being wrinkled, and with freckles too—Julia never could appreciate the men who came so regularly to Lily's apartment. But she was a good neighbor. "Look like you've been having fun yourself," Julia said.

"Nope. Too early for me yet. Plenty of time for me to get my bath, and fix my hair, and get ready for the customers," Lily said with a wide laugh.

Julia had never known another woman who seemed so unaffected with being a whore. "Alexander coming tonight?" she asked.

"Nope. He better not. That fart's been bringing me some real rough customers lately, and I'm willing to bet one or two of them were police. No, tonight I'm having company from Hollywood." Lily put her chin up in mock superiority, then added, "If everything goes right I'll be able to retire for life when they leave." Julia had to laugh with her. "But where're you off to?"

"Just going to get something to eat."

"By yourself?"

"As usual. Maybe I'll go to a movie too. I quit today, and am celebrating."

"Quit the school you mean?"

"Yeah. Mr. Plommer won't have to worry with me sassing him, and whacking his precious little hooligans anymore."

"That's the same guy we threw out of your apartment that night isn't it?"

"No, that was Clarence, the woodshop teacher. Anyway, I'm all through with teaching."

"What're you gonna do now?"

"Be leaving for Louisiana first thing Sunday morning. Going back home."

"General knows about this, or is it a secret?"

"Oh, he knows. When he gets out he'll come and meet me in Shreveport."

"Well, too bad you're not interested in making big money. Lots of fellows I know would be willing to take off behind you if you ever give the sign; but I have to agree, you know, your way is the best way. I just got off on the wrong foot. Don't suppose you're expecting anybody to come by or anything while you're gone tonight?"

"No."

"Let me keep your key then. Might need it if things get too rough over here," Lily said.

Julia felt in that moment a little sadness for the white girl. She went into her purse and handed over the key.

"Maybe if you're worried you should call Alexander and have him stay nearby, anyway. Does he know the people who're coming from Hollywood?"

"Hah! You crazy? If I tell him anything about them I'd never be able to retire," Lily laughed again.

"Well, I'll call before I come in," Julia said.

"Okay kid. Have a good time. And don't spare yourself if somebody really nice comes along—General won't even have to know."

Julia was undecided about where she would go for dinner. She had thought vaguely of some dim restaurant, maybe with candles and thick carpets on the floor, but the times when she had been in such places were very few, and she couldn't think of one to which she would now be attracted. She walked to the garage and pulled up the door, then on impulse shut it again on the shiny Corvair, and decided she would set out walking. At the intersection where her street met The Boulevard she turned up, and put the sun over her left shoulder. It was warm. Another smoggy summer day in Los Angeles. With its attendant roar and sweep of endless motorcars. This neighborhood was not too long ago white, exclusive, residential. But along The Boulevard now, the little taco and hamburger stands which seem to follow wherever black people settle in Los Angeles announced all that was at an end. Ray Charles on the jukebox. The smell of frying oil and hot spices. Laughter. A quick scuffle on the sidewalk between two fine men, who, it turns out, are not really fighting at all, as they stop to watch her go by, saying in false entrancement *"Mmm mmm mmmm!"* And the houses behind the stands double-storied pastel green, pink, and ivory smooth plaster, not the brick of eastern cities, didn't look so cold as they did when white people were here. Windows were open. Music, and colorful clothes hanging in the smog-laden breeze. Children, many children, on the lawns trampled brown, and the sidewalk, full of games and laughter. And if here and there a broken pane, or stripped gutter, or rusted wall, the frequent ambulance, police, and fire sirens hinted at incipient decay, the shells still for the most part were very pretty, and the children's voices very sweet to her ears. Why had she never enjoyed her third-grade class in elementary school? Why had she never enjoyed teaching? As if that were the same question as loving children! Julia passed on along The Boulevard, wondering briefly why Lily stayed. She was white. And somehow her voice saying When the first Negro families started moving in in '59 all the white people packed up and moved out. Not me. I was glad to see them go. I was so sick of my neighbors I didn't know what to do. You know the type —old farts who listened to Fulton Lewis Jr. all the time and turned up their noses at everybody. They didn't like me either, because I always had lots of boyfriends. So I said to myself, good riddance. Now maybe the kid will have some real honest-to-goodness people next door for neighbors . . . somehow didn't seem right. Honest.

Could it be, if Lily's boyfriends that she saw were all strange white men she would still feel the same? Suppose she didn't have to watch, not have, but watch just the same, one after another those well-to-do-looking black men going up to Lily's door night after night, and listen to them roaring off in Eldorados and Electras, would she feel the same strange mixture of friendship and hostility for the white girl? Lily was a dependable friend. That night when Clarence had gone beserk, unbelieving that she was in fact refusing him, when she couldn't stand it any more and ran to Lily's apartment, the white girl and her friend Mr. Alexander had stopped whatever they were doing and come immediately to throw Clarence's ass out. Mr. Alexander had his gun, and it had given her pleasure to see Clarence backing out the door whipped, stuttering and begging pardons. And Lily had advised her afterwards that she ought to get a man. Right here. Not one in jail. But for her, the episode with Clarence was enough of a fright to keep her lonely, because she did not want to imagine another man in General's place, since this seemingly would defeat her whole ideal in womanhood—which was to take and make a man fragile, then fill him with her own strength and make a world through him. She was on her way with General, and did not want to start afresh with anyone new. There were times when she wished to be as carefree as Lily. But there was a price on that too, which was in itself worse than an eighteen-month loneliness. And April was just eight months away, and she had quit her job and was going back to her family in Louisiana, and she was in her new red dress on her way to dinner, with admiration coming from a proper distance—whistles from the hamburger stands, and honking from the cars, even appreciative looks from a few of the women she passed on the sidewalk— and she didn't know where she would eat, but the evening was already her own event. Julia passed on along The Boulevard, feeling somewhat like the time when she was homecoming queen in Atlanta, only this time more certain of her power to bring changes into the world. A home with General, and the four boys her womb would give life to growing up to be strong men. An athlete, a musician, a professor, and a politician. And then perhaps a girl, who would be just like her—if not quite so lovely—just to show she could do that too. Julia passed on along The Boulevard, refusing to think about packing and making preparations for the long drive to Louisiana. Or closing the bank account, or sending a letter to General to let him know she would be leaving Los Angeles. She passed on, until being suddenly struck by an aroma of unusual spices when she came abreast of The Creole Cafe, a new establishment she had never noticed before. An aromatic blend like peppers and rosebuds, or something as strange but exciting. She went in.

There was no carpet on the floor. The black tile was polished to a high gloss that reflected her shoes, the slender cane-bottomed chairs, check-covered tables, and all the various shadows which shot in through the wide plate glass window which looked out onto the sidewalk. The light fittings were all bright brass. And the kitchen, if it could be called that, where all the cooking went on, was right behind a white counter against the back wall. But it didn't feel cheap. There was something cozy about the way each table had its four chairs neatly erect as though guarding separate domains of privacy. The cooks were two slim black men in stiff white smocks and chef hats. There was no music. The quiet private voices of the few patrons, and a quick laugh from one of the cooks which had a new melody in it. Julia felt glad she had followed her impulse, and looking around for where she would sit saw Mr. Alexander alone at a table in the corner away from the wide window quietly indicating with his eyes she would be welcome to join him. She did.

He was as usual immaculately cool in tan suit over a mild lavender shirt and tie. "Mind . . . ?" she said.

"The pleasure is only mine," he said. "You look beautiful. How've you been?" Pencil-thin moustache above his wide lips which seemed to have remained younger than the rest of his pale tight face, especially the eyes, gleaming like he'd been awake too long.

She took the chair opposite him saying, "Fine. How about yourself?"

"Me? I keep it quiet, until someone super like you comes along. Looks like you're on a heavy date, or something."

"No. Just came out to dinner, and maybe I'll go to the movies afterwards." He had never stopped eating. The same exciting smell that had pulled her in was strong everywhere inside the restaurant. "What is that you're having?" she asked. "It sure smells good."

"That's curry number three," he said.

"Curry?"

"Yeah. You never eat here before?"

"No. I didn't even know the place was here until I saw it just now."

"Curry is what they do here. These boys are West Indians. And until you taste it, there's a grand treat waiting for your tongue, your throat, and all your sinuses if you get the really hot kind."

"West Indians? They're not from Louisiana?"

"Nope. West Indians."

Bringing back the new music of the cook's laughter, and Julia said, "Hmmm!" A waitress came, and with help from Alexander, Julia ordered. "I'll try the medium hot," she said.

And turned to look closer at the cooks behind the counter, who were now talking to each other in a quick high melody that had feeling more than anything else. Easy. Pliant.

Mr. Alexander was finished eating. He pushed away his plate and lit a cigarette. "So how's the school business these days?" he said.

"It was fine, the last I saw of it," she said.

"What do you mean?"

"I quit. I'm going back home to Shreveport."

"All of a sudden just like that? Or is something wrong?" And before she could speak, "No, don't tell me. You heard from the man in Joliet, right? He's found himself a jailhouse Nancy to replace you, right? Heartbroken, you see nothing else to do, but go on back home to mother. Right?"

"Wrong. I'm just tired of being so far away from the people who really know me. And I don't have to be, so I'm going back."

"What about your friends here?"

"Who?"

"Well, Lily and me, anyway. Lily really digs you. And me, it's true I've only been to your apartment once, and you've never been to mine, but we've seen enough of each other in passing. And you're hip . . . You know I'd go in the hole for you if the time came." Mr. Alexander spoke very calmly.

"I guess so," she said. Then laughed.

"What're you laughing at?"

"Oh, I just remembered that night with Clarence, when you came in my apartment and pulled out your gun . . ."

"Oh, yeah. That dude . . . you must've had a spell on him his mama couldn't remove. He ain't the reason you're leaving town, is it?"

"No. I just had enough of Los Angeles, I guess. It'll be nice to be with Mama and the rest of the family again, and take it easy for a while. You know it's a strain making it in Los Angeles. You and Lily are okay, but people here aren't as warm as they are back in Shreveport."

"I don't really know, but I have a feeling what you mean. I've never been to Louisiana myself, but I've lived in Mobile. And whatever else they say about colored folks down there, they sure know how to take care of their own. I guess I really know what you mean. But it's tough to see you go—and us never having a chance to do anything together."

"Dinner at 'The Creole,' Mr. Alexander," Julia said, putting on a mock air. He smiled. She felt gay, and wanted him to know she wasn't really under any emotional distress. It pleased her when he smiled.

"You really are a beautiful something," he said. "I'm beginning to miss you already."

Julia's dinner came. Rice and peas, salad, and meat that looked somewhat like barbecue, but giving off that strange aroma that made her conjure up vistas that were never before so strong in her imagination. The Indies. Palm trees and blue skies. And new musical voices that made themselves felt without piercing.

"It isn't only that I could care for you, you know," Alexander said. She understood. "It's like, if you didn't have absolute strong feelings against it, I could help you set up here to be your own woman, anyway you like. Meet the best people, trips to Reno and Las Vegas, Mexico City, just about anything you want that money could buy."

Julia liked Mr. Alexander, and was admitting to herself that perhaps she always had—ever since that night he saved her from Clarence. But she couldn't help feeling right now a little sorrow about the game he was pushing. The food was good. The pepper was hot, but no more than she had tasted many times before leaving Louisiana. "Do they serve drinks here?" she said.

"Sure," he said.

"I'll buy. What do you want?"

"Uh uh! I'll buy." Signaling for the waitress, and continuing to say, "Look, Julia, business is the best these days. I'm telling you. With your mentality and the graceful way you got you could move out there and make yourself a thousand a week easy." Mr. Alexander, with his brand-new Continental which would be paid for in less than a year if only he could get two more girls working for him on The Boulevard or if Lily would push harder.

"What would you do with Lily?" Julia asked.

"Lily's fixed for life. Right now she doesn't even need me, so I won't have to do a thing with her. I'm concerned about you. Because I know you aren't like some women who would be thinking this is a nasty business, and look on it like they're selling their soul. A man when he wants to be entertained doesn't think of selling and buying. A woman neither. Only me. I must be the only one who would think like that, and I'm wrong when I do. There can't be no selling and buying where a woman is concerned, she does what she wants to do. And there is exchange to make sure she's got freedom to do what she wants to do. Now you take some women who talk about marriage like it's some almighty protector from everything evil in the world.

When they get married they're making exchange too. Only it's exchange into slavery. They ain't free to do what they want to do, and they cry about it, and weep, and first chance they get run off and content their heart, telling themselves what he don't know can't hurt him. Now that's a fraud. And it is true, like you know, when a woman gets into making fraud she get to be smaller, and smaller, and smaller, until she don't know where to find what she was looking to be in the first place. It takes guts to be a real woman. You got it. I can see clear as we're sitting here, how much you got it . . ."

"Well, thanks. But, you know, I have General coming home in April. I'm not exactly looking to choose what to do with my life, I've already decided. And I like it. You'd like General too, if you ever met him. Did you know he is a member of the Nation of Islam?"

"Oh yeah? 'S that since he's been in?"

"Since he's been in. They have a chapter, or whatever it's called, in Joliet, and he joined right after he got there."

"Oh yeah? That's cool. I dig those Muslim cats. If things were different I'd be one myself. But you know, there's a lot of hypocrisy in them too. General should watch himself."

"What's funny about the Muslims?"

"Nothing. Except I don't understand how come they're seldom doing what they say they're supposed to do, and always getting shot down or busted behind lightweight stuff. How come?" As though it were a question he expected her to answer.

"Maybe that's what they are supposed to do," she said, wondering did Mr. Alexander know that she felt a strong liking for him, the way one would for a tame squirrel or some such cuddly pet. A way she had never felt about General, who was man and muscle and commanded her.

"You know," he said, "I dig them. Really I do. I'm not putting them down. And if one of them comes to me and says 'Brother, I need fifty bucks,' or whatever, and I got it to give it's his. But I've been in jail, man. Yes I have. And I ain't promising to go back for nobody. Nothing nor nobody. Those white cops make a mess of a man if he stay long enough in jail . . ."

Alexander . . . It suddenly seemed he should have had other names . . . Promised to die before going back again to jail, but was

not above running girls on The Boulevard, or fishing from his cool
tan suit pockets in view of whoever wished to see from the remainder
of the restaurant an envelope full of assorted plastic pills, and another of cigarettes, and a third half-filled with grey powder which didn't
shock her at all even though she knew it must be heroin or cocaine or
one of those. "See this here?" he said. "Six good months of this and
I'll be ready to float down the Nile or even the goddman Mississippi
in style."

"For whom?" she asked.

"For whom what?"

"Six months of that for whom? Are you on that stuff?"

Mr. Alexander grinned. "Now looka here," he said, "do I look
like some sort of a fool to you? This here is for my customers."

"Boys here in the neighborhood?"

"No, no, no. I wouldn't do that. Besides, I like the big time—my
customers are all in Hollywood. I tell you, I'm on the inside with
people you wouldn't believe . . . movie stars, politicians, musicians,
big-shot businessmen, you name your style and I could deliver it to
your doorstep . . . lined up at your door and you in luxury here, in
Acapulco, wherever you want. And that'd be cool. Because you,
where you are right now, are a luxury that few men have ever laid
eyes or their hands on." He put away the envelopes and lit another
cigarette. "But you're leaving town," he said.

Mr. Alexander was ugly when he over-lied or pleaded. But in the
main there was a magic about him Julia did not want to cast aside.
Surrounded by the warm aroma of The Creole Cafe, separated from
the after-work Boulevard still going by outside the glass window,
Julia felt it was useless to deny his fascination. To her he was like a
little intense animal newly broken from the wild that reminded her
how in her faithfulness to General she had been regularly undermined not only by frightful dreams but by her own body which since
she had been alone had not stopped getting lovelier, and even now
throbbed with tenderness it seemed malicious to conceal. Not because of Alexander's come-on, but because of all the things he didn't
say about what he would never have. Couldn't she see that ten years
from now when she and General would be one-third owners of their
home, and the eldest son winning his first prizes, Alexander would

still be on a beat like this? Hustling to be poetic before a pretty woman? Even after the bones of his face stood out clearly, and he should be in a rocking chair with maybe pet canaries whistling in his ear—if he lasted that long—still hovering on borrowed time between the prison and the hospital, carrying his grave beside him? She had not read Baldwin for nothing. Nor ignored the tremors beneath her heart every time she heard sirens in the neighborhood. Julia smiled, remembering dimly in a juvenile past her vow to be no man's solace for the sake of just that, smiled at the contentment imagined in this moment at being just that—solace to this man, or a black other. Smiling silently at him, Mr. Alexander, terrified man, his terror leaking through the got-it-together exterior and masculine cologne to penetrate into where she knew there was peace, completeness. Wasn't he desperate? Weren't they all desperate, these black men? Living life a cutting edge, forever being honed away for—what? And she, Julia, a little afraid too. Not because of some vow to be no man's solace, but from standing so close to losing all or not growing. Laughing at these intimations she said, "You are a joke." Laughing, but accepting whatever it was he slipped into her hand with a "Here. One for the road." Accepting, with a sudden fierce decision to show him trust.

It must have been good, whatever it was, because although he kept on talking she wasn't hearing a word he said. On the mist of exotic pungent aromas going back to the cane brakes of Louisiana, and the smell of sugar syrup and molasses, and voices from the chain gang somewhere over the hill singing

> Be my woman gal, I be your man
> Every day a Sunday, dollar in your hand.

Julia felt like singing. Hadn't felt like singing seems like since she was a teen girl walking home past the street corner—

> See see rider, see what you done done
> Made me love you, now your man done come

with a passionate heart determined that men should love her with or against their will, and she would have babies, and babies, and babies, until the world was fully, undeniably the fruit of her womb.

Every last bit of it the fruit of her womb. "Do you have any children?" she asked Mr. Alexander.

"Five," he said. "Oldest one twelve years old. I love them."

"Is their mother jealous?"

"Five babies, five mothers," he said. "And I love them all—babies and mothers. Why? You ready to have some babies?" Which must have made her smile, because he smiled and asked, "How many?"

"I feel like singing," she said then. And he, gallantly, "I know just the right place where you can sing all you want, and maybe you be another bird. You hip to Bird?"

"Oh, yes . . ."

"Man, they say Bird dead, but I know just the place where he's living so hard his feathers growing big like plam leaves and everybody in that place floating. You ready?"

They took to The Boulevard, then, in the calm of early twilight, stretching the success of curry number three straddling down the lanes, past Western Avenue, and pointed east with the sun already down or coming up in Africa, just as you pleased. Past Vermont, and Mr. Alexander himself relaxed with his stingy brim over one eye and his manicured nails smoothly elongating the Continental, so that without having left where they were it stretched them in a curve back west past Crenshaw and other names, past plaster houses and people standing quietly on the street, under patchy clouds in a sky docile, and perhaps a little weary. Under a concrete arch in an asphalt driveway, hearing the clanging bells of the streetcars, and catching sight of a heavy-bosomed grandma massaging her breast and piecing together a wrong story in her eyes—Julia had felt sorry after thinking her bitch—but a wrong story, nevertheless, even though he had returned to the car whistling Bird, jaunty and free for any turn, and slid it like a whisper forward into between two others, and had in a drench of suave cologne helped her float higher into the room. What followed after that was unclear.

Julia slept late. A sleep better than any she'd had in a month, because there had been no dreaming until dawn, and then of a lovely green sea that had given her its sweet water to do with as she pleased, and gold-striped fish, and fire-red corals, all under her command, as were the waves and wind-song. She heard the telephone a long ways into time again, before coming through her eyes into the room where a mid-morning sun already slanted through the venetian blinds. The mirror pulled dust-beams from the window and slashed them down again across the empty fried chicken takeout paper box, a glass jug of water, the empty Champale bottles, and the drinking glasses still in their sterilized wax-paper covers. She was alone. The telephone rang again, only now coming distinctly from the radio on the bedside stand. It must have played all night. Following the telephone came a voice which reminded her of what they used to call at home a white preacher, saying, "This is K-Pawk. Are you there Mrs. Muldane? Mrs. Muldane, are you there? Yes, yes, This is K-Pawk, and all you have to do to win today's super bonus prize is tell us the name of the song we just played . . ." Julia switched off the radio, and the room became quiet.

As in the dream of that beautiful sea rocking to her rhythm she was alone, but it felt good to have had such a dream at last. Unlike the others which had been coming so steadily, so hard of late, in which strange brutish men picked off her limbs, her breasts, and other parts of her that were not flesh and could not truly be named but hurt just the same. They had been so steady of late, until they had come to seem real. Like history, or the story of one's future viewed in advance. Julia did not want to remember those bad dreams, nor the ones in which General was ripping off some foul behind in a jail john, because he wasn't superman and a body in hock makes strange demands. Julia couldn't think which was worse. But tried her best to call back slumber in the bed, cradled in the memory of warm waters, undisturbed by the litter on the chest or her dress crumpled beside the bed, or her scattered underclothes. It was a terrible test put upon them, her in Los Angeles, General in Joliet. And she closed her mind against recalling what it was like during summers before they took him away. Above all, though, they had promised to be honest. And she made a mental note this would be one of the first things she would tell General when he returned—how she spent a night with Alexander. She could afford to. She felt purged. It would have been different if the feeling was she had sinned.

The telephone came again, to be the real thing this time, and when Julia answered, she heard Alexander's voice. "Hey, baby,

What're you doing still in that place? Don't you know what time it is?"

"Who is this?" she said, letting it be venomously known she did not like being disturbed.

"Who . . . whoo?" he stammered. "This is Alexander."

Without another word Julia hung up the telephone.

She smiled to herself in the warm bed thinking, wouldn't it be fine if this really were a blue ocean far away and she on it reaching some corner of the earth that was pretty with flowers and green trees, and birds, and laughing people without motorcars, and easy lovers who did not struggle so hard to vent sperm. Easy lovers who understood a woman's fancy for sailing, and consequently never felt they were the one to bring her dead to a standstill.

Julia remained in bed for a while longer, daydreaming about being home with Mama, the hugs and kisses, and how they would handle a shopping trip to New Orleans. And there would be men in Shreveport, and New Orleans and everywhere with whom she wouldn't feel bashful or intimidated, or threatened as she did in Los Angeles, where she had several times thought to buy a gun, or knife, some weapon that could spill a man's blood. People in Los Angeles pretended too much at being hard. And came at you with the intention to break—she didn't know why. Maybe because there was so little rain in the city. No nearby woods. Too much the smell of gasoline. Julia remained in the bed, very pleased to be on the verge of leaving the city. Until it seemed she was overdoing it. Then she got up, stretched luxuriously, went to admire herself in the mirror, and brush her hair, and decide that a shower in cool water was what she wanted. She was a long time taking her bath, scrubbing carefully. She had no lotions or creams for her skin, but brushed her hair again. She had forgotten her lipstick too, but was pleased to see that her lips had a nice color all the same. Julia finished dressing and left the motel. She felt good, and could have a nice time the rest of the day packing.

On the morning of August 12th Los Angeles was hot and humid. The temperature was past ninety-five degrees, and the sky was trying to live up to a professional forecast of rain. Give it credit, the sky managed a dark cloud or two, but no rain came.

ROUTINE ARRESTS OF THREE SPARKS MELEE

one newspaper headline said.

On the morning of August 12th, the rain which might have come to Los Angeles had already been expended four days earlier in a place called Americus, Georgia, upon a famous Southern politician expounding "I am tired . . ." of running he claimed, and surrendering, and compromising. Standing in the rain before more than three hundred Georgia hard necks all joined in solemn desperation turned valor, announcing in a voice chorused by the heavenly water their suicidal stand for honor, glory, translated in the cry "protection of our rights."

Perhaps it is every man's duty to die for the protection of his rights, and kill a few others in the process as well.

There were those in Los Angeles who believed the same. Given not the rain of a Southern county, nor the cant of homespun politics; given but the brazen flow of blood from their own heads, which every man woman and child suffered in truth, memory, or expectation, the black people of Watts were on the 12th passionately uprisen in a post-rational battle against the devil in their lives. He wore white faces. Uprisen against hunger and spiritual frustration, against the non-vision which made no distinction between them and garbage in the street—except that they bled, garbage didn't, which made them excellent nutriment for all ailing egos.

RIOT UNCONTROLLED!

WHOLE BLOCKS IN FLAMES—DOZENS OF WHITE
MOTORISTS BEATEN

SNIPERS SHOOT AT FIREMEN—POLICE UNABLE TO
CONTAIN CROWDS

WATTS BARRICADED

The newspapers broadcast nightmarish accounts of a terrible demon threatening to engulf the city—

God! It's terrible. We're just sitting here praying.

I saw three cars turned over and burned and two Caucasians

beaten by Negroes.

God, it's terrible.

I am a respectable woman, and never have I heard policemen talk like they did last night.

You goddamned right I threw bricks!

I threw bricks and bottles and anything else I could get my hands on.

White devils! You started all this the day you brought the first slave. You created this monster and it's going to consume you. You can't hold it. You can't let it go.

On the morning of August 12th, Here come whitey! Get him! a cry in Watts, where there had been no rain all summer long, and the heavenly blessings associated with this life-giver from the skies seemed but dreams of an ever more remote design. The black sons and daughters seeking to purify their lives stoked great cleansing flames with their nothings, dared lethal weapons with their nobodies, crying "We have nothing to lose!" And a white man said, "Never have I seen such a look of pure hate on their faces. Something has made these people awful mad."

Julia never paid any attention to headlines. As she boarded the bus on her way home the driver made it a point to touch her hand while returning her change. "Shouldn't be out here without protection," he told her. His fingers were thick, and although he was already bald, there was an intensity in his face, a hint of extraordinary vigor in the shoulders of his starched uniform. He wore a pencil mustache, and altogether reminded her of a brown boxer she had once seen when General had taken her along to see a championship bout at Comiskey Park. Julis smiled. "Be glad to be of service after I get off," he said. Julia without answering passed on into the bus. There were just five other people, all sitting separately, and she did not look at any of them closely. She took a seat beside an open window but soon changed. The air which rushed in when the bus moved was too hot, and smelled too strongly of something burning. Otherwise it was a pleasantly sober ride, quite opposite from the feeling of unfurling and passing into a new liquid state as had happened in Alexander's car the previous evening. Once when Julia looked up and caught the driver eyeing her through the rear-view mirror, it was pleasant to feel his eyes, but she had nothing to return him. At her stop, she was about to step down when he said, "I get off at three o'clock. What's your address, huh?" She walked off without turning her head. The heat was strong.

"Jesus, I've been worried about you," Lily said, when Julia got to her apartment.

"What for?" Julia stopped at the door.

"What for? Christ, people're getting killed and beaten up all over the place and all you could say is 'what for'?"

"Who's getting killed and beaten up?"

"Where the hell've you been? I knew I was right yesterday evening. Where you been, some rich pad up in Hollywood?"

"That's hardly my style," Julia said. "Who's getting beaten up?"

As if she couldn't already tell. As if a sudden emptiness hadn't formed inside her, and a prickly feeling break out all over her skin.

"The niggers're whipping the shit out of the police in Watts, and, you know, the cops are jumping everything black they could jump on."

"Who're the niggers you're talking about?" A little red noise had come up in her ear, and soon it would penetrate into her whole head.

"Ah, shit. This ain't no time to get sore. The police are getting their asses kicked for a change. This ain't no time to get sore."

"Where is my key?" Julia said.

And it didn't matter that Lily hardly looked like a whore today. Her hair was combed back quite simply from her forehead, and caught with a plain clip at the nape of her neck. She wore loose slacks and an innocent blouse. For once dressed, but not made up. She could have passed for a suburban housewife. But Julia's head was filled with quick shadowy images, and her heart was racing. Lily while rummaging for the key was still talking ". . . Liquor stores, furniture stores, pawnshops, everything. The people are taking over. Goddamn it makes me feel so glad! You should've seen those suckers last night when the news came over the radio . . . Got their hats and split for the hills like frightened rats . . ." She was laughing. "You should've seen them . . ."

The red roar exploded in Julia's brain like a whiplash, but she forced herself to be steady. She stepped inside Lily's apartment then, and closed the door behind her. As usual, it smelled ugly—stale cigarette smoke and aerosol deodorizer. Julia made herself sit down on the shredding couch and said, "Guess you didn't have time to make a killing, huh?"

"Oh, I did all right," Lily said. She found the key. "But you're right, I didn't have time to make out like I wanted to." She laughed. "How about you? Must've been a damned special movie to keep you out till damn near midday."

"Oh I decided to skip the show."

"Where'd you go?"

"A motel."

"By yourself alone?"

Julia was beginning to enjoy talking to Lily. "No. I met a very nice man."

"Well hurrah!" Lily said. "Did you make out?"

"He was a very nice man," Julia said.

"Is he going to come by? You going to let me meet him?"

"Oh, nothing like that. As a matter of fact, I won't even be seeing him again. Besides, I don't want to have too much to tell General when he comes home."

"Oh, shit—General, General. That sucker's in the can. No telling what he's going to be like when they let him out. I'm glad you finally got up and had a little fun. I don't see any need for you to stop now."

"Oh, I'll be having my fun," Julia said, "Don't you worry about that. How about Alexander, did you hear from him?"

"Did I ever! I believe that pimp's got some Jew in him." Lily hadn't stopped turning around, and now she produced two cups of coffee. They sat sipping. "First thing this morning he's ringing my doorbell, coming in here with his eyes on fire. 'Okay bitch,' first thing he says. 'Come on, where's the bread?' Just as though he was standing right here while I made that two hundred and fifty bucks last night. I says to him, 'What bread?' But I could see already he was set on getting tough. So . . ."

"He didn't let you keep any of it this time?"

"Nah. He was in a real nasty temper. Took a while for me to make him civilized again. But it's okay. He went off someplace shopping. Said he would be back before long."

"Wasn't he worried, with the police jumping on people and everything?"

"I don't guess so. He knows what's going on."

Lily offered her a second cup of coffee, but Julia refused. "I guess I'd better start packing, if I'm going to leave this town on Sunday."

"You're really going to go, eh?" Lily said.

"Oh yes. Come Sunday morning me in my little Corvair will be out of here headed for the Southland."

"Christ," Lily said. "I can't see why you'd ever want to go back to a place like that. Doesn't all that segregation and stuff down there bother you?"

"That can be a bother, all right. But it will be nice to be with Mama and the rest of the family again. And, who knows, I might even take a little vacation trip down to the West Indies."

"Oh, *that's* where he's from."

"Who?"

"This nice man you met last night."

Julia laughed. She got up. "Well, I better get over and start packing," she said.

"Why don't you wait until Alexander gets back?" Lily asked. "We could get him to take us over to Watts so we could see the action. Wouldn't that be a gas? Imagine—the police getting their asses kicked. Man, I would really enjoy seeing that."

The shadowy images returned. And the strange roaring noise began to fill Julia's ear again. "Well, I'd better be going," she said.

"He'd love to take us," Lily said. "They have police barricades and all that, but Alexander is a card. He'd love to show us how he can handle the police himself. I'll call you when he comes, and maybe you'll change your mind about going."

Julia left without answering.

Inside her apartment there were letters on the floor. The telephone bill, light bill, and a letter from General. She put the two bills on the counter near the kitchen sink, and took the letter into her bedroom. She turned on the radio. The Negro station to which she kept her dial turned was not playing music. A strange voice pleaded,

"Brothers and sisters, it is in all our best interest for you to remain calm. Please remain calm. The police are not our enemies . . ."

Julia kicked off her shoes and sat on the bed, then decided not to open General's letter. It seemed better to be doing something busy. She opened the closet, and swept an armful of dresses out onto the bed. She started picking up shoes, and throwing them at random on top of the dresses. And then, against her will, she slumped on the floor and began to cry. The red noise filled her brain. The black shadows became clearer. She had no family in Watts, and General was away in Joliet. Yet she cried. Her womb constricted until it hurt, as she envisioned the policemen grouped, weaponed, faceless behind helmets and goggles, marching. Marching upon hordes of black women, children, and men in foul clothing scavenging smashed stores, and the streets and sidewalks littered with broken glass, bits of paper, rags and debris. Hearing the voices, the angry voices of harassed black men, desperate women who tonight, if not dead, would be somewhere groaning inside the pain of broken heads and arms and legs, and shot-away stomachs.

Julia suffered as though every wound were hers, as though the pains were not only sharp, but old inside, as though they belonged with the bones. Then after a while she felt nothing. Neither worried, nor sad, nor terrified, nor even pleased that at last black people were rebelling. She found herself wondering if the West Indies was a safe place to raise babies.

In a little while the doorbell brought her out of her dreaming, and it was Lily again, still dressed as before, and directly behind her Mr. Alexander saying, "Hey, sweetheart, how're you doing—you sweetest thing either side of the Mississippi?"

Julia smiled. They came in.

"They have the army on standby now," Lily said. "I just heard it over the radio. Isn't this a gas? Makes me feel good all the way into my womb."

"Nobody wants to hear about your womb, female," Mr. Alexander said. Wearing a fresh cologne, and some grey slacks with a blue shirt of sheer silk, and being almost regal in the way he looked down on the two women. "The bloods in Watts is kicking ass and that's what's happening. That's all. Now if you want to go down and see some of the action, I know just how to handle that."

Julia smiled. "Don't think I want to go," she said.

"The army's on standby," Lily said. "What's the matter with you? You don't even seem interested. Aren't you glad your people are standing up at last? Aren't you glad?"

"Look baby . . ." Mr. Alexander said, but Julia did not let him finish.

"Glad about what?" she said. "That a whole lot of black people are going to get killed? And many more crippled?"

"But they're standing up," Lily said. "I'm not a Negro and it makes me feel glad. Just like I felt when the Jews caught Eichmann —and I'm not a Jew either. It's got to make you feel some kind of pride when your people fight back."

"Looka here," Mr. Alexander said, "you chicks're going off into something that don't even matter at all. Now the Captain of the 77th precinct and me, we are tight. That dude knows me, and if I want to go into Watts and check out the scene, all I got to . . ."

"Why don't you stop being such a goddamned ass," Julia exploded. The roaring was in her head once more, only this time it would not be contained. It made her feel red all down her neck and arms. "It doesn't bother you this is going to end like all the others?" she said. "By tomorrow morning there's going to be a whole lot of black men and women killed. Dead! To be raked up off the streets like yesterday's trash. Doesn't that bother you at all?"

"I never would have believed you would talk like that," Lily said.

"That's because you expect me to be just another dumb bitch," Julia shot back. "And none of the dead bodies will belong to you. You could afford to feel glad 'all the way into your womb.' That's probably the only way your womb gets to feel glad—when our men, black men, are getting their heads blown off and you think it's for you."

"Julia, I think you're losing your mind," Lily said. "If I was black I'd be willing to get killed too rather than live the way niggers have to live in this country. Right now, today, I wished I was black. I'd be down in Watts. Not up here, talking about leaving town . . ."

"You could afford to say that cause you ain't black," Julia said. "You go to Watts and 'check out the scene.' Go get your womb full.

Ain't going to be nothing but dead bastards in it anyhow . . ."

"I thought you two chicks were tight with one another," Mr. Alexander said. "Now cut out this hassling, and let's get on the road. I want to see my bloods in action."

"As if white people aren't suffering too," Lily said. "We get hurt. And a lot of white people got beat up on Avalon Boulevard last night. How about that . . . ?"

"Serves them right," Julia said. "And you too, if it would've been you. Because you take a black man between your legs every now and then you think you know what it is to be a black woman? You've got to believe somebody's giving up his life for you. Well nobody dies for me, you understand? You go and watch the police blow away those black men in Watts. Not me, you understand? I am meant to give life, and I intend to be life-giving . . ."

"Still you shouldn't say it serves white people right to get beat up," Lily said.

Julia suddenly felt at ease again. "Well it's true, isn't it?" she said calmly. "Anyway, I've started packing already and I don't want to stop now."

"Say," Alexander said, "you really going to be leaving town for real?"

"Sunday morning," Julia said.

"Say, I was thinking . . . step outside a minute baby," he said to Lily. She hesitated. It was plain to see that she was close to crying. "Step outside," he added, when she had not moved fast enough to please him.

Lily started towards the door, and Julia took a step or two behind her, until Alexander grabbed her wrist. Lily went out quietly and closed the door behind her.

"Look," Alexander said. "After last night I figure we ought to talk a little more before you really make up your mind to leave town."

"What about?" Julia asked.

"Well," he said, releasing her wrist, "I was thinking you're just the, you know, sort of girl I've been waiting on to sort of settle down with. I can take care of you. And I know you can take care of me . . . I think we can do all right. You know, nothing extravagant—a house in Baldwin Hills, trips back east every now and then. Kids. I'd like you to think seriously about that."

Julia smiled. "Do you really know the captain at the 77th precinct?" she asked.

"That's strictly business," he said.

"And how about Lily?"

"She's strictly business too. Look, you know what's happening. A man's got to make it the best way he can. There ain't no such thing as dirty money."

Julia hardly heard him. Her thoughts had begun to slip off again, only this time there were no mutilated shadows, no noises in her ear making red visions. She thought of a warm playful sea, and herself at play in the blue water with white birds passing overhead but too high to be anything more than specks on their way to a distant island. "Do you have your gun?" she asked.

"In the car," he said.

"Then, why aren't you in Watts fighting the police?"

"Hold on, baby," Alexander said. "I ain't about to go get myself killed, now. I've got a lot of living to do, and I aim to do it. Mostly with you."

"I've got a lot of living to do too," Julia said. "And I'm going back home come Sunday morning to wait for General. April isn't very far off."

"And what about last night," Alexander said.

"I'll tell General about it."

"Everything?"

"I'll tell him everything. He'll understand. He may even explain the full meaning of what happened for me."

Alexander was silent for a while. Then he said, "I should've met you, say, five or ten years ago. If things don't work out after April, you come on back to L.A."

"Maybe," Julia said. She was tired and wanted him to go.

"You want me to go, don't you?" he said.

"Yes. I have to start packing."

He took her wrist, and tried for an embrace. But she did not give herself.

"Well, tell Louisiana hello for me," he said.

"Be careful," she replied.

In the Winter Of

In the winter when he showed signs of feeling pulled down Julia had suggested that he take himself out for a night on the town. He did, and had a dull time, but lied when he came home saying the sights and sounds had cheered him up. Julia seemed pleased; and he congratulated himself on having saved her feelings. Within a week she had made the suggestion again, and before January ended Juju's night on the town had become a standard device for siphoning off possible explosion. They had come close to wrecking each other in the past—or rather she had come close to wrecking him and felt duty-bound since their renewed promises to see the tearing did not recommence between them. And perhaps if she had not been pregnant they would have gone together sometimes, but she had to be careful, and that she felt included her staying off the streets, particularly at nights.

As the spring came on Juju found he liked the Jazz Workshop best. He had been patron at many bars and nightclubs along Fillmore, through Chinatown, and on the waterfront. None compared with the Workshop. It remained one of the few places without acid rock music and topless dancers, and he had twice spent the consecutive nights of a whole week listening to Coltrane there. He was not a heavy drinker, and, since settling with Julia, seemed to have lost the will to seek other women. In all his rounds he did not make any friends. At the Workshop he found the kind of music often enough that not only made his loneliness cherishable, but revived confidence in it being fundamental to anything beautiful which he might discover or create.

Julia was pregnant with his child.

In May, she was round, and truly getting heavy. He was sure he loved her, but became more restless in his considerations of her feelings. After a day counting money in the bank on Montgomery Street, he usually took a detour that brought him home in the dark. Julia was supreme in her patience and never complained if he ate the dinner she had waited without looking at her or saying ten words, then took to the streets again.

"Think I'll go down to the Workshop for a while."

"Be careful. Do you want me to press a new shirt for tomorrow?"

"No. I'll change on Thursday."

On Tuesday night Juju had a choice. He could go to the Jazz Workshop, or he could visit Callie. In all of San Francisco within ten minutes of Nob Hill, or the glitter of Fisherman's Wharf, or Chinatown, or Haight-Ashbury if he wanted either, but the choices with meaning were Callie's apartment, or the Jazz Workshop. He had outworn the other places. Art Blakey and The Jazz Messengers on a Tuesday night made very good sense. There wouldn't be too many people, and he could get a good seat and listen without too much in between.

Jazz alone would have been the choice if Callie had not earlier that day come into the bank, straight to his window, in a swirl of black cape and lavender skirt minnied almost up to the crotch of her stockings. She being the kind of woman that caught your senses even without such a getup—smallish, but with all her copper smooth-skinned self a single flow. When she came close enough leaning on the counter her grey eyes flowed like glazed marble. "Haven't seen you in a long time, Jerome," she said. "How is Julia?"

"She's well."

"So am I. Even if I have to be doing it mostly by myself," she laughed. "Julia's lucky."

"Are you still planning to go home for the Independence celebrations?"

"Right now Trinidad is the furthest thing from my mind. I have

too much to get done here. And you know what? I might soon become a restaurateur."

"Really! Where?"

"On Haight Street, possibly." Talking on; a bluntness in her voice
letting him know her case of desperation was over. She being no
longer the same woman asking him two weeks ago to "make a raid.
With twenty or thirty thousand we could start a good business back
home . . . I'm sure you could find a way. You're a Trinidadian,
man." Today she was Callie, high-brown sweetheart from Port-of-
Spain with the man-world knocking on her door: who, though not
bred in Carenage or Diego Martin could have married a Huggins or
a Fernandez—men of substance and class, you understand, if you're
from Trinidad. In fact, one of the things about even university men
in America was that they had no class, most of them. Talcott was different. This new find was really brought up in Canada and therefore
a gentleman: in some extraordinary line of business which may not
be revealed, but rich enough to buy her a restaurant. Not an eating
house like what most black people run around San Francisco, but
something on the order of what Left Bank artists might have patron-
ized in the Twenties. Evidence—a five-hundred-dollar deposit to her
account in one bill, to be followed, of course, by the thousands neces-
sary for investment purposes.

"Where did you meet Mr. Talcott?" Juju had asked while making
the entry in her passbook.

"You wouldn't believe it, Jerome . . . one of those meetings you
scoff at all the time. One of these days you'll see with your own eyes
the kind of benefits that come from mystical enlightenment."

Which he dismissed as usual, since Callie had had many finds before—men, books, movements—none of which had proved substan-
tial enough to liberate the Cinderella in her. "So when are we going
to see you?" he had asked.

"Not tonight. We're having a meeting at my house. On second
thought, why don't you and Julia come by?"

"You know I don't go for any of that mystical thing. Maybe we
could see you after the meeting is over."

"If Ronnie and I don't have to go on campaign afterwards."

"Campaign?"

"To cheer up lagging members, and encourage new people to join."

"That shouldn't keep you past eleven."

"If you really want to be with me tonight you should come to the meeting. I can't promise anything."

Talking like that: no longer confessing loneliness. Gone the time for camping out in their living room, their kitchen; leaning on a countryman and his woman.

Why not? If she had really found a fairy godmother. Wasn't he seeking one too? But don't call it that. Self-realization. A unified and fulfilled self. What's the difference?

There was a slight mist about the eucalyptus treetops as Juju crossed the Panhandle. Here and there flower children were gathered in pairs or groups on the ground. Where caught by the street lamp's glow their dull white faces were gaunt, often grimy. Faces he passed two or three times each day but which did not know him: faces without concern for what he thought of the rags their owners wore, or the matted hair in which they were mostly hidden.

"These hippies are like pigs," Julia had once said, in a moment of vehemence rare for her.

"They have a right to be the way they please."

"That doesn't mean shit. They around here pretending to be on their asses, all they are doing is making things harder for people who are really in need."

"There's a difference between the poor and the hippies. These are giving up things real poor people never come close to having."

"Just the same, they want the same thing as everybody else— peace and happiness. Only they don't want to work for it. Who do you think supports them?"

Not that he had wanted to argue with Julia anyway: feeling as he did, that she spoke of her own confrontation with unhappiness. He didn't care what the hippies did.

Yet as Juju crossed the Panhandle between them sprawled on the ground singing, or playing their guitars, or smoking, or making love, a strange sensation turned inside him; and if he were not a rational man he would have rolled in the dirt and invited himself to share a joint, or stormed among them violently kicking in their bellies and stomping the half-visible faces.

Callie too. Who had no right making him feel he was being left behind because he denied her mysticism. As though in spite of four
years at university, and his name in plastic on the teller's window he
still was a long ways from having found out how to live beneficially.

Juju, give Callie her game.

Which would have been easier if he didn't feel the need of something to push against.

At Divisadero he could take the Mission bus that ran by Callie's
apartment; or he could take the downtown bus that would bring him
to the Workshop. He was undecided. Fortunately, neither bus was in
sight and he didn't have to make an immediate decision. A radio
from the corner store outside which he waited was loud with voices
that were either the Beatles or some group like them. The sound
made him feel more intensely the need for his own music to bring his
head in touch with both viscera and feet.

The Mission bus came first, but Juju was not quick enough. In the
moment while he hesitated over what to do the driver had dipped
quickly into the stopping zone and out again, and in a split second
Juju was watching the tail lights going sway through the intersection.
The downtown bus was not far behind, and this time Juju was quick
and firm in boarding it. The bus was near empty. At Golden Gate he
transferred into one emptier still, which gave him full moment to
study himself mirrored in the opposite window. Not bad. To look at.
High-shouldered but not bulky, and a young boy's face if he smiled.
Without the smile, high-shouldered but not bulky, with a young
boy's face under a pall of reluctant manhood. Or that might have
been just his imagination.

The night breeze was sharp along Market Street, and changing his
mind about riding the open cable car Juju took the Stockton Street
bus up to Broadway. The bus was so crowded he had to stand, and
somebody at the back played a harmonica. Many of the faces were
young and cheerful. Some looked like American holidayers he remembered landing in Port of Spain—festive, transfixed, overflowing
with subliminal romance. On Broadway, fashion-plate couples
strolled past the cafes, mingling with others who still dressed for the
bohemian North Beach underground of a generation ago, and still

others who wore leather jackets and square-toed cowboy boots. There were long queues outside the topless places, and a good crowd gathered around one cafe that had its dancer shaking tits in a second story glass cage overhanging the sidewalk. The nightclubs were all brightly lit with neon blinkers and other decorative lights, and at one corner the crowd moved slowly between the music of a belly-dancing bistro across the street and the ringing banjos of a dixieland bar with its doors wide open.

Exhilarated and lifted a little out of himself Juju kept walking towards the Workshop. The faces belonged to strangers, but there was a general kinship in the atmosphere, and Juju felt something close to excitement being pushed or bumped against in the warm crowd. Suddenly, it was not an accident, someone laid an arm firmly around his shoulders, and he looked up into the grinning face of Mike. Big and warm, grinning widely, his half-Indian face full and cheerful in the light, Mike said, "Where're you going, boy?"

In an instant the years rushed back, and Juju couldn't help himself saying "Goddamn!"

"Yeah. How've you been, my man? Haven't seen you since the last flood in Iowa."

The crowd kept them close, but did not make them give way.

"Goddamn! Mike!" Lifted completely out of himself for the first time in months it seemed, he hung on Mike's big hand with both his own. "Man, where are you coming from?"

"Live here. You headed for the Workshop?"

"Yeah."

"Come on. Let's breeze back and dig some sounds and catch up on what you been doing—little mongoose."

Which he hadn't heard since the time when somebody thought he was to be the next 200-meter world champ. "What are you weighing now?"

"Two seventy," Mike said.

Juju pushed off his forearm against whoever was passing them and said, "Let me see what you can do over fifty."

"No, no no. Too heavy for you baby. You got to make it longer than that if you want to taste my dust. My momentum alone would kill you."

They laughed.

"Come on. I'll buy you the first drink of rum you've had since that winter in Iowa, I'll bet."

"I ain't going for that." The big man dropped his arm around Juju's shoulder again. "You West Indian niggers always want to make somebody drunk."

"You Apaches just ain't got no head."

"We were the first jazz musicians in the world, though." They laughed, jaunty and light until they came to the Workshop.

The swing sign outside announced *"Art Blakey and The Jazz Messengers."* There was no line waiting, and they walked right in.

The band, they could hear as they entered the Workshop, was not Blakey. With a wide choice of seats because there were no more than ten people in the club, they sat over against the wall, ". . . so we won't be in the direct line of this fire," Mike said. A petite brown-skin waitress came to get their orders, and Mike asked, "When is Blakey coming on?"

"He didn't make it," she said.

"Didn't make it!"

"No. We got a call, and they're hung up in Vancouver. But they'll be here tomorrow night."

"Damn! Who are these people?" he said, indicating the band-stand.

She appeared not to have heard and asked again, "What would you like to have?"

Mike ordered Scotch, but Juju was a little disappointed and he could sense his feelings go down as if a stopper had been pulled on them.

"Goddamned police!" Mike swore.

"What do you mean?"

"I bet some hick town cop's trying to get famous offa Blakey."

"Busting him?"

"Yeah. Those cats travel with their stuff on them. Can you imagine, some Canadian cop walking up to Blakey or one of the boys and finding something on them?"

"I've always heard Vancouver was a liberal town. The Canadians aren't as harsh as Americans."

"That's a myth, man—like the fearless cowboy. There are no de-grees of harshness when it comes to white policemen dealing with black musicians."

The pick-up group from Oakland was very bad. Two black gui-tars, a white drummer, and a trio of female singers. Juju didn't even bother listening when the MC announced their names. They looked serious, but the guitars and drums, the voices, did not touch his feel-ings.

Like so many days in Iowa, which he could still visualize if he wished, but which had gone by without feeling.

The guitars were loud; the voices high and frenzied. Urgency there, in a mechanical way. "Don't they remind you of the Tender Trap?"

"That place in Cedar Rapids?"

"Yeah."

"At least that group there was trying to play jazz. I don't know what these people are trying to do."

"I don't either; but they seem very serious."

"Yeah, too serious. Seriousness belongs to the dead, man. That's the beauty in jazz . . . Being very serious about not being serious. But these kids don't have it. They're all dying young."

The Scotch was cheap and bitter. "Don't talk about dying," Juju said. "Lately I have spells where that's all I think about."

Mike grinned. "If I remember you, that means you're having some kind of woman trouble, right?"

"No, no. Not this time."

"Don't tell me, nigger. I remember when that pretty one from L.A. . . . ."

"Julia?"

". . . yes, Julia, left you in Iowa and you almost lost your mind. So don't be telling me not this time. Who is she?"

"How about you, are you married yet?"

"No, not married. My woman's out of town, and I miss the hell out of her. Are you married?"

"No, Julia and I have an apartment on Fell Street. You've got to come by some time. She's pregnant."

"You two finally got together, eh?"

"Yeah . . ."

"Boy, do I miss my woman," Mike said. "I do," with a far-away look gathering in his eye.

Wouldn't it be fine if he Juju had that to say? Where had his feelings gone, for Julia, Callie, anyone, so that sitting next to Mike he could observe his friend's lament, but not feel it.

"Where is she?"

"Visiting her relatives in St. Louis."

"She wasn't in Iowa, was she?"

"No. I met her after I came back to California."

"She a black girl?"

"No. She's white, but she's okay. I tell you, I've gone through a lot of women, but none of them had what this one's got. Helen isn't pretty, either. But man, there's nothing phony about her. Nothing. She is for real in everything she says and does. I miss her."

"Julia has folks in St. Louis too, but we've never been there. Let's have another drink," said Juju, signaling to the waitress. "When is she coming back?"

"Should have been back already, but you know how these family affairs go. She's only nineteen."

Which didn't seem too young to Juju, or just right, or anything. No picture, no feeling. Thinking about Callie, and saying, "If you're really strung out I know a chick . . ."

"I know lots of chicks. That isn't the question. When Helen gets back you'll have to come over and meet her. We're living on Potrero Hill."

"And what're you doing?"

"Teaching, man. I'm over at the J.C. teaching P.E. And you?"

"At the bank. I'm a teller these days."

About which they laughed, recalling days in Iowa when neither one could lay fingers on a ten or twenty. "And here you are fingering that man's money every day. Thousands of dollars, I bet."

"But fingering's all. I can't use any of it."

"I know they keep an eye on you."

"I'm the only black man in the bank. As I go, so does the race." They laughed.

When Mike suggested taking themselves away from further musical abuse they sauntered out again to Broadway; and after a big airy place with topless dancers, and another with female impersonators they decided on going to his place on Protero which Juju half-heartedly did not want to do. More certainly he did not want to break the trance of Iowa recalled, days which in memory were more alive than they had been when he lived there. The melancholy pastels of fall, white winters, and the first warm days of spring when they walked through town with their jackets open. The pride with which—at times—they wore those jackets emblazoned with the track insignia, and the crowded stadium within which they stripped their limbs bare for Juju to race 200 meters, or 400 meters against the Big Ten's finest, and Mike to hurl the javelin and discus, and put the shot. Days of surviving together in basement apartments with scarcely enough heat, and toilets two flights overhead. Landlords and coaches and town merchants, all seeking their profit in you; and women, whom Mike in those days disdained, and Juju seemed perpetually unhappy about.

"It really is nice that you and Julia finally got together," Mike said as they rode off Bayshore in his Mustang. The car was black inside, and Mike's eyes were fixed alertly on the road and he leaned with the wheel in places where the road curved. "I always thought she was a good girl."

"She's all right."

The factories and warehouses of South San Francisco were dark, and they passed very few cars along the way.

"You better marry her this time, man. Not for her so much but for the kid, you know. We black men haven't been taking care of business where our kids are concerned."

"I'll take care of the kid."

"But you don't really want her anymore, is that it?"

"Hard to say. Sometimes I do and sometimes I don't. I think she is unhappy about it too."

Mike drove over the hills and around the corners with much feeling for the road, making a very fluid ride. "She is a good girl. I remember her going off with that crazy cat in Iowa, but you were a fuck-up in those days too, you know. Carrying yourself like you were something specially God-given to the race."

"That's all past. I don't have any hangups about her and other men."

"Oh, no?"

"Not from the past, anyway."

"You're damn right! That cat . . . what was his name? . . ."

". . . General . . ."

"General, he had a hell of a game going, and you didn't have shit. You lost in the semi-finals that year, didn't you."

"Yeah. That was a bad year."

"You should've won that race. But General was a bitch . . . all that black identity stuff. Iowa City wasn't ready for that. Did he ever get out of jail?"

"He's back in again." Visualizing General—bearded, small, and dignified—with much feeling akin to love, and aversion too; and a touch of anxiety remembering some of the scenes Mike did not know had passed between himself and the little exhorter.

From Mike's apartment on the hill the great picture window looked east towards Oakland. The night was misty still, and the golden lights of the Bay Bridge curved away in the dark without sparkle. Mike brought two big drinks in from the kitchen. The phonograph was already going, and Coltrane's quartet sounded very alive and powerful. The music cut across Juju's remembering. In the music Juju could feel where he wished to belong, but he had no picture. It was a great distance away, and he would have to travel. Mike stretched out on the floor, and Juju sat propped up against some cushions. The music was sweet, sometimes melancholy sometimes furious, but hinting always at a peace beyond the next few bars. Mike turned over on his back. Juju stared out at the lights. If he had to go on a long journey he could not take Julia—or anyone else for that matter. What would he say in explanation?

"There's this chick named Callie," he said.

"Yeah? What about her?"

"Picked up with some white cat who she says going to buy her a restaurant."

"You dig her?"

"She's from Trinidad too; but I didn't know her there."

"What is she to you?"

"Nothing."

"Then leave her alone."

"She is something to me. I feel like I should break her."

"I knew you had woman troubles. Can't stay away from it, can you?"

"You know, I don't want to hurt Julia."

"Nigger, why don't you settle down?"

The Scotch was good. It made Juju's mind turn very keenly, almost to the point of bringing in pictures. Callie was a mystic. Julia, since she came to donate herself heart and soul, he had difficulty feeling. She was like a warm emptiness in which he turned. "You mean work my way up in the bank, and buy a house, and all that?" he asked.

"Why not?"

"Is that what you plan on doing?"

"I'm not going to leave this gig unless I have to. And as soon as Helen comes back I'm going to marry her, and take it from there. We've got a lot of stuff to do. You dig Trane? We've got a lot of stuff to do, and I can't do much of anything if I'm playing around."

"I'm not playing around."

"Yes you are. You must be, or else you'd be talking about what you're laying down for the future—not about breaking some chick you only halfway know."

"Well, maybe if I could see a future I'd be doing something about it; but I don't feel much of anything out there. I can feel what I want it to be like, but I don't see much of anything out there."

"Can't see it until you make it," Mike said. "Why don't you come and teach at the J.C.? It will be less of a hassle than any bank. Give you a way to pull yourself together and time to lay down something. Every day I deal with those young kids out there, I understand more clearly how critical it is for me to really put down something. I know you can get on the staff for September."

"The bank isn't too bad; they leave me alone. It would be nice to have all your vacation, though."

"That's right. We have another week before summer begins, and if my woman isn't back by then I'll be on my way to St. Louis to find out why."

"Yeah."

"I really miss my woman, boy, I really do. Be me and that Mustang across the U.S.A."

"Maybe if you go to St. Louis I'll ride with you," Juju said on impulse, the picture taking shape as he heard the words—himself beside Mike on a long fluid ride, slow, and beating the wind in their faces.

"Thought you said your woman was pregnant."

"She's only six months. We'd be back before the baby comes, won't we?"

"I suppose. But it sure would be cold to leave her alone."

"It won't be for long, and her sister is supposed to come up from Louisiana to spend some time anyway."

"Well, that's up to you," Mike said.

It was after midnight when Mike offered to drive Juju home, but he refused. He felt strong and expansive enough to walk all the hills in San Francisco. Just the same, at the base of Protrero he stopped at a phone booth and dialed a cab. He was neither unhappy nor unfeeling, waiting in the damp night for the taxi to come. He felt very pleased at not having gone to Callie's; and it didn't matter that rich and semi-rich white kids were right now under the Panhandle eucalyptus trees making love, or that he might encounter them there tomorrow night or the next still making love. He felt firm and strong, and the feeling lasted all the way home.

She was waiting for him in the new bathrobe which was his Mother's Day gift this year. He felt strong enough to talk to her, maybe even hold her hand. She didn't move away from the television program she was watching, but her eyes followed him through the door. "Did you have a good time?" she asked.

"I ran into Mike," he said. "He's just as big and friendly as ever."

"What is he doing here?"

"Lives here now. Teaches P.E. at the junior college. I never knew whether I would see him again, the last time he left us in Iowa."

"The last time he left you in Iowa."

"Well, me. How are you doing?"

"The baby kicked three times while you were gone. One of these days maybe you'll be around when he does, and you'll get to feel it."

"How do you know it's a he?"

"Kicks like it. Was the music good at the Workshop?"

"Terrible. Art Blakey was supposed to be there but he didn't show and they had some rock band from Oakland."

He wanted to say to her the word lovely. She was lovely. Her natural brown tone seemed just a little flushed, and he loved the softness which pregnancy had brought to her face and eyes. If he touched her she would be soft, and warm, except over where the child made a high hard mound at her middle. The softness flowed even into her hair which he touched saying, "How is my little Louisiana Creole?"

"The doctor says I should get some more exercise," she said, "or else I will get too fat and the baby might become overgrown. What do you think?"

"He said you should get more exercise?"

"This is my sixth month, and he said I should do more walking. I really felt like it tonight too, but you hardly said two words when you came home from the bank."

"Well you don't need me to get more exercise, do you?"

"But it's not safe walking in the neighborhood, Juju. And pregnant as I am I couldn't do a thing if somebody attacked me."

"It always comes down to someone attacking you. Who's going to attack you? For what?"

"Just today the woman in the apartment house next door was beaten up two blocks down the street. Some man took her purse and smashed her in the face. You think that couldn't happen to me?"

"Well . . ."

"Let's go to the park sometime, Juju? We could walk there."

"You could walk there by yourself."

"Not in the dark."

"What's wrong with the daytime? All you do is sit here in the apartment—except when you visit the doctor."

"If we're together I won't be afraid."

"What's to prevent someone from attacking me?"

"I'm not afraid of that. You stay out all the time and never have any trouble."

"Let's walk together in the Panhandle then."

"Okay."

"You're not afraid of the hippies?"

"I won't be afraid if we're together."

Realizing all the while that was just what she had wanted—a promise from him, a commitment, obligation. Against which he must lie, or cheat, or falsify in order not to fulfill. He was not going to walk anywhere with her.

So why not tell her so?

Juju withdrew from the living room and went to bed. He could hear Julia waiting for him to get settled, before she turned off the television set and came in herself. She hung her robe in the closet and joined him in bed. She was wearing the perfume he had given her for Christmas, and a great lump of anger formed in Juju's chest as he caught the smell. He relinquished practically all the cover, and drew to the far side of the bed hoping she would not speak. But she did.

"What's the matter, Juju, is it too warm?"

"No, I'm okay."

"If it's too warm I'll turn off the heat."

"No."

He could feel her leg cross his, then she said, "You are warm. It's no trouble, I'll turn off the heat." Leaving the bed, raising her round body in the low reflection of the night light to adjust the thermostat —when that wasn't it at all. Just him. In a fury without explanation. Loving her but gelid against it, against any feeling except anger driven out the pores and making him sweat even though the room was not uncomfortably heated.

So it made no difference what she did—tend the thermostat, dry his sweat, or even say she loved him. The thought of her doing each shot his fury higher, and it took all his will to lie hands clasped between his drawn-up knees when she returned to bed, his back to her, hoping she would grow still, or retreat, or best, just disappear like a shadow. Julia did not deserve this.

That Old Madness—1974

Everyone's thinking we're gone back into the pen these days, but let me tell you right now, I one mad mother. People don't really believe that. But one of these days it's going to come out boiling and I'm going to get me some notches on this gun, baby. I *know*. Sometimes I have the urge already, and when it is very strong I could almost feel the pulp of dying throats between my fingers. Like this nasty morning. The sky showing no consideration for human beings. For three days it's screwing up a dirty grey face and belching shower after shower of rain. It scowls and gathers down like somebody up there's trying to force a new fear into people's soul—but I am not afraid. I laugh at those clouds trying to make like it was The Flood again. They don't reach down to where I walk. And the unfriendly wind too. Drives a stinging rain, and brings cold swooping down from the snow hills. And all through this I must walk, must work. Of course I don't work under the open sky, but by the time I walk through the pelting rain with the sky playing such stupid tricks, I am ready when I get to the bank to fling people's money at them and dare with a dead eye anyone to tell me how much the new swimming pool cost, or how long the children's been in hospital, or what a bad day they had at the races. Once some clown even started telling how at thirty-five he had to be paying for his own circumcision—until he looked up into my eye and saw what was happening. He ducked his head and shuffled off. They complain to the manager that I am unfriendly, and some pretend not to see my window. Suits me. They are very right. I am unfriendly. I am worse than unfriendly. When the day comes, and I start to kill, I won't know them from anybody else. Especially those pompous ones who think they're doing you a favor handing up some filthy money to be in their *savings account* for three days—until the weekend. Handing it up like they buying the Empire State, for the man to make his ten percent and hand them back three or four. Like the big real estate boss. His mother was probably black as the ace of spadro, but he's a *real estate* boss, cigar and all, dig it? "Well young feller, how're you getting along? They treating you right around here?" "If they aren't, what you gon do about it?" I asked him. "Why," he said, "I do believe you mean to be sassy. I'm one of the oldest customers here now, and I'll have to talk with the manager." When I got through counting I chucked his money so it fell off the counter, with a lot of half-dollars rolling under people's dresses and behind wastebaskets. If it could have shown he would've turned red, but as it was he just turned blue and blustered, "You nhgger! You little nhgger . . . !" Trying not to say "nigger" too plain, and glancing over his shoulder to see who might be overhearing. The manager ran out from behind his desk and helped pick up the money. Couldn't help notice how look-alike they were—slick-haired, dry-skinned, shifty-eyed, and when the manager's newly back from Puerto Rico—couldn't find much difference in color either.

They all say I am cold and unfriendly, and they are right. What they don't know is that one of these days I'm going to rake all that money out of these drawers and start running—only so they could try to catch me. Then, quick. In a single turn around. *Poppity pop pop*, baby. Like that. Ten pins; or just the way they did the Indians. These people don't have any *idea* how angry I am. Some'll say I stole and killed because I'm a nigger and these are things niggers naturally do, others will say I am mentally deranged, others will say I'm weak-minded (which amounts to the same thing) and there'll be those who believe Satan had possession of my soul. They will *never* think of me being angry. Angry, angry. Who's talking about being angry—that lameness of a past era? I am talking about getting free, mother. Totally, calculatingly *free*. They will never believe that I who am trapped in their city—the greatest (pen) in the world—had it in me to shake so free. And to tell the truth, even I'm not so sure sometimes. But I know I *am* black: those others be white, and the thing between us is here. People carrying on like they don't see the signs—they're *insane*. Laying the burden on me to get things straight. All right. I could be insane too. All the villainy comes my way, I could make that into the best kind of madness. I *am* mad. I got this madness strong enough to taste from my tongue all the way into my lungs. And it don't know no strangers.

Only yesterday, coming through the sidewalk water, with the wind damn near buckling my legs, and one of those *regulatory* signs saying *"Don't Walk"* holding me up with a host of cars waiting. I could see this man and woman (white like snow—or maybe ivory) settled comfortably behind their wheel, and their little future president gazing at me out of the window. "Hey, boy! Hey, boy!" That was him. Practicing for the glory days. Hey boy—after all the fires and blood of so many centuries. Sent madness racing in my veins so, my nose got warm. What business did he have calling out at me so cheerfully, like I'm one of his playthings? When I fixed his pink Sunday-morning face he glowed and waved "Hey boy" as the car pulled away. Then a curious thing happened. Before I knew what I was doing my hand jumped out of my pocket waving in return. That was disgusting. But in a way all right too. One of these days my hand'll jump out and be waving in return, but not empty. Be getting me one or two then, baby.

Everywhere you turn around you hear them saying "Times have changed, haven't they?" Then out trots those ready evidences—black capitalism, minority representation, right-on power to the people and all the rest. Like if that's where money comes from. (Whatever happened to Tommy Smith? What's become of his children?) Hey, somebody's gon say, Look at you. You're doing all right. Why you're a teller in one of the biggest banks in America. Which is cool—until we start looking at what it took to get me there: two college degrees (nine years of my life in adult education detention), a bunch of credit-account clothes, some grammar and a body language which camouflage the best in me, and a daily reverence to some incognitos who purportedly know best how the human soul is to express itself. Machines, baby. If the machine can't handle it, then it is extra whatever it intended to be. Right? And ask them, ask them when am gon make VP?

Course, now, that's a different matter, you see mister blackman, we have people here much ahead of you in experience with handling money (college degrees is just a minimal qualification). Why, even some of our female tellers have more experience than you. Yeah. And, of course, you can't fault a man for hiring his boss' son. Or a friend's son. Or a friend's friend's son. Wouldn't you do the same thing if you were in that position? All right. So the issue is clear. Only, before you can do anything for a friend you've got to free yourself of your enemies. Not so? Okay—hey boy. The black youngster on the other side of the fence had something real for me when I smiled and waved cheerfully at him. His eyes popped wide, then narrowed, and with a stiff shoulder he turned away. Not back to play, just away—and what's to stop me from feeling guilty for ruining his moment? I'd be a fool to say Don't know, now. Wouldn't I?

On the bus it was different, but no better. People did not turn their heads away, but the blank and indifferent stares insisted upon my nonexistence. Me, I take on shape and form, become recognizable as a nuisance. Or a danger. Even children know that in order to defuse a nuisance all you need do is disregard it. Dangers, of course, are to be eliminated. All right. I sat next to a grey-headed old man who kept twitching his coat, and pressing further against the side of the bus, and I crowded him. Not because of the madness clogging my throat. Not because I felt provoked enough to smash him down and stomp him into a pulp. Nor even out of any wish to taunt him. But discipline. Hundred percent discipline. He gave off a foul and musty smell, and I hated him for it—even as I knew that after my walk I too smelled hot and musty. I hated him for smelling; I hated him for daring to remain seated next to me and not know how readily I could strangle life out of him. I hated him for looking human. But, discipline the first foundation: timing the major principle.

When I got up to leave the bus I was careful to smile at the old man in a most friendly way.

Inside the bank I was a terror. Nasty to customers, and the supervisor who kept giving me hints on how to get along with people. He's on the list too. I hate the whole bank—the manager who's short and semi-bald, and looks like an uneasy reformed bandit; the supervisor who is working his way to the top by being friendly with everybody; the women. Most of all I hate the women. There is one who has been "with the bank" for twenty years. Has fingers look like giant maggots. When she speaks, the entire building rattles. And there are others. The young ones who think I have nothing better to do than want to get in bed with them and therefore be making clear how improbable such an achievement would be. Everybody here thinks I am a pushover. All right. But I laugh every evening when I load the heavy trays of currency into the vault, with the supervisor smiling his "good boy" smile at me. Because, one of these days he will be very shocked when he turns around and realizes that his good boy has made off with all his good money. He will turn to follow, and that's when it'll start—*pop pop poppity pop*—and the neighborhood papers will put that down to my having come from a race of sub-intelligents with a sub-cultural, underdeveloped, fatherless, deprived background.

Sources

Early Morning

About five miles east of San Fernando on the way to Princes Town lies a village where a red-topped church sits before the cemetery that slopes humpily down to the railway tracks. Next to the church stands the school, and after that come little painted houses crowded so closely along both sides of the road that no more than a quick glimpse of the canefields which roll away from their backyards to the rim of the sky is permitted between them. At the center of the village there is the square, an oval of pastureland where football and cricket are played, and where the men not on shift at the factory gather in the shade of scattered mangoes and almonds to talk and cut each others' hair. The square is bordered by the post office, police station, and two rumshops, and behind these stand small clusters of tin-roofed cottages where most of the villagers live. Eastwards the village elongates again, finally ending about half a mile from the factory.

At this point the road forks. Black and narrow, the asphalt main road rises through Jaipaul, the abandoned Indian settlement where overgrown posts, decayed outhouses, and many gnarled mangoes remain the only signs that people once lived there. The main road goes past the dairy where Satan's bull Thunder once roamed, then curves between the fields away to Princes Town. The other arm of the fork is a gravel road stretching down between tall palms to the sugar factory which is surrounded on three sides by upward folds in the land. This factory with smokestacks taller than any tree in the countryside rumbles day and night from January through June each year, and between six and seven every morning during crop-time the workers walk, trot, or ride their bicycles in a thick safari down the palm-lined road—some to relieve those coming off the graveyard shift, others to disperse into the fields.

Descendants of slaves and indentured laborers, the dark, gaunt crowd of undernourished men and women make their way down the straight gravel road, with much cajolery and laughter. Their clothes are little better than rags; yet they appear hardy, long-suffering, capable of enduring extreme hardships down to the very day when their flesh will dry up, and their bones collapse. But on occasion, when some father can no longer face the stares of his hungry children, or some young man's love elopes to the town to become a maid or streetwalker, the despondent father or heartbroken lover slips off from his house in the dead of night armed with his rope and grease, and the following morning he is discovered hanging from a tall mango in Jaipaul, dead, released from the despair he could no longer stand.

So it is some mornings as the village prepares to meet the seven o'clock whistle, the milk boy comes in from the dairy raising a great cry, "Dead man in Jaipaul." The villagers hasten their dressing and rush to the scene. Beyond the junction they converge upon the tree where the corpse hangs. If it is raining they cover their heads with sheets of old newspapers, but if it is a clear morning with the sun still pink as a baby's palm, they stand or squat in clusters along the roadway staring at the tree. Rain or sun, and whether it be neighbor, father, or brother hanging dead, no villager approaches closer than six feet from the dead man's tree.

He must come down, but the villagers know that anyone crossing the six-foot boundary takes a step into the kingdom of darkness, a step few are given to withdraw. They know that the dead man's spirit is condemned to Satan's kingdom, for the zone of darkness lies just on the other side of life, a desolate realm of perpetual anguish into which all suicides inevitably pass. A cacophony of screams and lamentations, an eternity of stumbling from one agony to another await all who enter there, and no captive may pass out of the kingdom without first bringing the master another to take his place. In its first twelve hours only the suicide's spirit is free to find itself a substitute, and the villagers know that during that time they are safer beyond the six-foot boundary.

The suicide's body must come down, but immunity against its frantic spirit is given only to one of them, and the villagers send for Samuel. As the sun gets brighter more and more men set their bicycles aside to stand in close knots about the tree; women and children hurry up from the village, the gathering grows and the constable has a hard time keeping a path clear for the buses that pass through on their way to the oilfields. The suicide's relatives stand apart, his son or youngest brother in the nightshirt there was no time to change, his mother or wife weeping, but even they stand six feet from the tree and no one moves an inch nearer before Samuel comes.

It is a nervous wait, but talk though not solemn is low. A few young men who rail against waiting for Samuel because they are brave and ready to take his job are restrained by the old ones who remember Ramjohn. He was a very brave man, a husky Indian with a fierce moustache who feared neither man nor spirit. At one time it was his job to get down the suicides, and it was worth an hour's pay just to wait and see him lift his heavy body smoothly, swiftly up between the branches like a big monkey, swing deftly to the dead man's branch, and bring him down under one arm. It was worth losing an hour's pay anytime to see Ramjohn scoff at the kingdom of darkness, walk in, walk out, as though none of the archdemon's wiles could trap him. Then one day Ramjohn slipped. For no reason too, because he was not a drinking man who might have been awakened from a drunken sleep, and there had been no rain to make the tree slippery; but midway through the performance he had carried out so well many times before Ramjohn slipped. No sooner had he gathered the dead man in his arm than he came down crashing through the leaves in front of everybody and broke his neck. It is given one man among them to walk in and out of the kingdom of darkness, but nobody knows when he too might be taken right before their eyes, so the villagers wait for Samuel.

At a quarter of seven when the siren sounds its preliminary call the workers grow restive. The sun is already drawing the day's first sweat, and the timekeeper with his pencil and pad is waiting to score the late. As the blast dies out above the treetops the workers no longer contain themselves; they begin cursing Samuel for taking his time, and fresh messengers are sent to make him hasten. Some slow children are chased off to start getting ready for school, and a few men pull their bicycles from the grass. The curses grow louder, more offensive, but no one crosses that six-foot mark and the hung man dangles there temporarily neglected; for the workers gather not so much to see the victim of last night's despair, not to feast their eyes on death, but to witness a man among them face the demon as no other dares.

When the first ones see Samuel approaching the junction they pass the word, and steadily a hush returns to the crowd as the unhurrying man in khakis shuffles on beneath a flop-brimmed hat. His clothes hang carelessly with the belt buckled like a vagabond's at the side. His skin is black and coarse; a crooked nose and split lip tell he has seen much violence. Samuel's bare feet are thick with the toes spread wide, and his eyes gleam small and red in the folds of his dark face. Those villagers who call him crazy watch with mixed faces as he enters the crowd; they do not know whether to admire or fear him. Samuel takes his time, he speaks to no one. With an ease belied by his clumsy appearance he climbs the tree and does a skillful job. After he is done the villagers hurry away to their jobs and homes chattering contentedly, all except the old ones who take their time to the shady almond trees in the square to lounge and take measure of Samuel's courage over again, from the time he was still a boy at the village school.

There are not many people in the village who have seen the devil face to face although there was a time when the demon visited nightly, inhabiting his favorite bull Thunder. In those days Samuel was just a lad of fourteen in his last year of school, and like everyone else he shivered each dawn when Thunder's shrieking roar split the quiet in which the village rested. For powerful as he might be, Satan falters in the face of pure light, and that trumpeting bellow of Thunder's signaled the moment when the devil had to begin his retreat before the coming day.

The boy and his father lived alone. The old man, who had accidentally lost a leg at the sugar mill, was sexton at the red-topped church, and he took great pride in his office. He kept the church clean, and tended the flower garden before it, but above all he was punctual about ringing the bell each day at six in the morning, twelve noon, and six in the evening. Many villagers who had no clocks depended upon his bell to get to work on time, and mornings when the sexton got up too late to strap on his wooden limb, dress, and get to the belfry on time, he roused his son and sent young Sam, who could run very fast in those days.

At six some mornings it was still dark, at six Thunder had already torn the air with Satan's voice, and at first Samuel was afraid whenever he had to run from his house to the belfry. Women on their early way to market had so often been scared back home by the marauding demon that at that hour Samuel had the road all to himself, and mostly he ran straight as an arrow, never daring to look around for fear the devil might be grinning over his shoulder.

However, as the run was completed many times over without any interference from the devil, Samuel's fear grew less. Eventually he even began to grow brave, and when the old father's chest could no longer take the morning air, Samuel, with only the slightest qualms, took full responsibility for ringing the first bell. As the months passed the boy's courage grew until the day came when he ceased running to his job. No longer holding his eyes straight ahead in fear, Samuel awoke to the sights and sounds of the late dawn. He heard the owl's last hoots mingling with chirps from freshly awakened finches and keskidees; he noted the sky, the stars that shone more cheerfully than they did at night. He looked deliberately at the shadows along the road, considering which would more likely be the one behind which the devil lay, and Sam thought sure he would be brave enough to face the demon if ever the moment came. No longer whistling or singing tremulously, in his thoughts Sam often mocked and dared old Satan to show his face.

As an altar boy Sam never missed a Sunday in church, and at communion services he looked like a black angel in his red cassock and white surplice, swinging the incense, snuffing candles, carrying out all the duties altar boys perform. He was Reverend Todd's favorite and had free run of the parson's library. He could read better than some of the first-year teachers at school, and practically every day after classes he lodged himself in the reverend's house reading books that were seen nowhere else in the village. Sam was not a stupid boy; thus when he found himself thinking "I'm brave enough for Satan—so brave he's scared to come at me," the boy knew he should have some corroboration for such untested boldness and decided to talk to his father about his thoughts.

That evening as the old man lay trying to hold back his coughs Samuel asked, "Pa, isn't it true that Satan's afraid of some people?"

The old man looked at his son. "Satan's not afraid of anybody, but lots of people are scared of him."

"Were you ever scared when you walked the road every morning to ring the bell?"

"Lots of times when I first started, but after that not so much."

"Suppose Satan had ever come for you, what would you have done? You can't run fast like me."

"Boy, the devil is powerful, he won't waste time after a one-legged old man like me. I found that out one morning couple of years back and I never told anybody because I felt ashamed of myself."

"What happened?"

"Well, I was going through the churchyard to the belfry when all of a sudden I saw a light coming down into the cemetery. It didn't come fast or slow, just floating down business like as though it knew where it was going. The first thing I did was turn to run. I wheeled around and took two steps, but before I ever got started I knew it was no use if that really was the devil after me. The best thing I could do was start to pray, so I stopped, leaning on my crutch with my heart leaping like a frightened frog and started the best prayer I know. I didn't stay like that a minute, I turned around to face whatever that demon was going to do, but when I looked, the light wasn't there. I stopped praying and looked up at the sky and down in the cemetery, but there was no light nowhere. I didn't know what to believe, until it struck me I'd let my imagination see that light. I knew right then my imagination had caused me to see and hear all the scary things that had kept my heart in my mouth, and that was the last time I felt scared."

"How come you never told that to anybody before?" the boy asked, for whenever villagers gathered in the square, or rumshop, or their homes, they spent a good deal of time comparing stories of their encounters or near encounters with the devil. Everybody heard Mary Lou the fisherwoman scream that morning the devil barred her on her way to market, and she too had seen a light, a green light; only it was like a flash of sulphurous fire that had blinded her and melted the road where she stood. Samuel himself had seen where the road had been melted and put back together again just as if nothing had happened. "How come?" he asked his father.

The old man lay back and stifling a cough said, "Shame son, shame. I'd spent too many years talking about Satan, being frightened at every strange sight and sound, when there was no need to be."

His father's words did much to strengthen Samuel's thoughts about himself and the devil, but he said nothing more to the old man. The following evening he approached the priest in whom he had great trust. He entered the study where Reverend Todd was working on a sermon, and after the parson set his work aside the boy asked, "Reverend, how come Satan scares some people and not others?"

The reverend laughed and said, "For the very reason God blesses some people and destroys others."

"But God blesses those that love him. Nobody in the village likes Satan, yet he scares a lot of people."

"That's not what I mean," the priest said, and he lowered his head in thought. He was a foreigner who did not believe much in what the villagers knew, and he always talked in roundabout words. Soon he raised his head saying, "God and the devil dwell in every man. He who nourishes the devil experiences the fear and distress which mark the devil's works."

The reverend's words were still not clear to Samuel, and the boy asked, "Doesn't Satan live in the kingdom of darkness? He's not really inside everybody, is he?"

At this the priest became impatient and asked abruptly, "Have you ever seen Satan or any spirits at all?"

"No," Samuel replied, "but I can feel them—especially when I go into a dark room."

"But if you had to find your shoes in a dark room you'd enter with a light, wouldn't you?"

"Yes . . ."

"Exactly. Light nourishes, brings to life the good things in the room and chases away the dark. So is it within our hearts. The kingdom of darkness is not a country somewhere on the other side of the world, it is a small place in our hearts. We each carry our private kingdoms wherever we go—in our hearts."

"With Satan and everybody in it?" Samuel asked.

"Satan and everybody else whom you place there. But the kingdom of darkness can be wiped away through faith in the truth, belief in God's word."

The priest continued with another long explanation to which Samuel listened with only half an ear, and when the man paused Samuel asked the question that was really on his mind. "Would a brave man die if he saw the devil face to face?"

The priest, who had subsided somewhat, answered, "Not unless he weakens son, only if he weakens . . ."

"And if he didn't weaken?"

Reverend Todd smiled. "That's a charge we should all carry, day after day," he said. "To see Satan face to face and not weaken."

After Samuel rang the bell that evening he started home through the dusk firmly convinced he was brave enough to hold the devil at bay, and Satan knowing this had avoided a confrontation. Sure if ever they met face to face he, Samuel, would have no fear. Like a warrior intoxicated with his sense of fearlessness, Samuel longed to put himself to the test. Nor would he await the devil's approach on some morning run to the bell; he would meet the demon face to face like Ramjohn, who in those days hugged the dead men on Jaipaul's mangoes like a bold giant.

Samuel went to bed early that night, and before Thunder's frightening roar stirred the following dawn he was up. He dressed and slipped out without awaking the old man. There was no late moon, but the usual morning stars glinted low in the sky as Samuel struck out through the village for the dairy. At the junction he took the asphalt road which curved through the abandoned settlement, beneath the mangoes that stood like ponderous shadows. On his way to find Thunder, to catch the devil leaving his bull, Samuel marched like a David already assured of overcoming Goliath. He would look the master demon dead in the eye and stare him down.

At the dairy he left the main road and swung into a rutted trace that took him across an open pasture towards the field where Thunder roamed. The morning breeze was cool, and the dewy grass wet Samuel's legs as he trotted on. He followed the trace down to a gully where tall canes reared all around, and with total disregard for the scorpions and snakes that breed profusely between the thick stalks Samuel crashed through the canes in a direct strike for Thunder's pasture. At last he emerged next to the wire fence which surrounded the bull's field. It was still too dark for Sam to make out anything but shadows in the field, and he paused waiting for some sign that would tell him which of the humped indistinct shapes was the devil's bull.

As Samuel stood peering beyond the fence his blood cooled rapidly. And despite the occasional fireflies that lit up for brief seconds in the distance, the fields and sky seemed gathered and silent. Samuel lifted a strand of the fence and stepped through. There were no early birds; the shadows, unlike those along the road to the bell, were formless and dense. They seemed alive enough to touch the sky, sometimes bunched in low menacing waves. They changed shapes constantly: his eyes could master nothing. And in all the coiling darkness around him and above, Samuel was alone. The realization struck home—alone. Somewhere in the shifting shadows was Thunder, perhaps nearer than he thought, and Samuel's courage began to fade. The determination and fearlessness with which he had left home were gradually displaced by a fascination that held him fixed, despite the shivery warnings he sensed each time the darkness billowed or sank. The cool breeze played upon his exposed neck and slid beneath his shirt. Suddenly Thunder roared.

Samuel felt the gushing breath of the beast slap his face, and with a cry he jumped back through the fence and bounded for shelter between the canes. Frightened, feeling very much alone, he began to cry. He was a long ways from everyone he knew, and the whole darkness seemed surcharged with an evil power that sought him out. Sobs came, then Samuel wailed, raising his voice louder and louder, wishing someone, anyone, would come to his rescue. When there were no more tears Samuel moaned drily, still crouched in the canes.

Thunder roared, his voice coming from across the fenced field, and Samuel moaned less loudly. He could hear his own whine, and suddenly he realized how unheroic it was to cower among the canes when the bull was nowhere near him. Again Thunder's roar came, from far in the distance, and Samuel felt ashamed. Quickly straightening up, he walked back to the fence and looked out across the dark field, but he could see nothing. He stood for several minutes while the dark morning became edged with grey, and still he did not see the bull. Finally turning about, he started for the church and his daily duty at the bell.

It was more than five years later when Samuel related his adventure, and then only after Ramjohn had made his fatal slip. The morning was dry and sunny when the Indian fell, and as he lay twitching on the ground with the dead man in his arm, the villagers gasped, yet none went forward to his aid but the young Samuel. As though this were a moment he had long awaited, Samuel was out of the crowd in a flash, straightening the Indian's neck, prying the dead burden from his arm, but it was too late. Ramjohn kicked his last and died before the crowd, even as Samuel was wrestling with his arm. When the youth looked up, the villagers were staring at him, waiting to see the kingdom of darkness receive its third victim for that day, and when Samuel walked away alive, they gave him a wide berth. Fully twelve hours went by before anyone approached to congratulate him for his dashing defiance of Satan and the kingdom of darkness. He was immediately regarded as having filled Ramjohn's place, and when some villagers asked how could he be so brave, Samuel puzzled them with "I know the devil, he knows me." Later on that night when he was drinking with some older men, he told them what the words meant.

Samuel's father died soon after the son started getting down the dead men from Jaipaul's mangoes, and the boy gave up ringing the bell the very day his father passed. He had already stopped attending church and, in spite of all the reading he could do, apprenticed himself to the village shoemaker. In time, that shoemaker passed, and Samuel now fills his office too. Never a talkative person Samuel has grown more taciturn with each passing year, and nowadays he seldom speaks to anyone. About his contest with the devil he never speaks, but he gets drunk often and whenever he does there is sure to be a fight with the man nearest him. Many of the villagers say Samuel is waiting for the devil to face him again, and this time it would really be a tussle to the finish because Samuel would be ready.

So on a morning before the sun comes up, when the milkboy enters the village screaming, "Dead man in Jaipaul," the villagers run out to see the corpse and messages are sent to Samuel that he has a job to do. As the sun rises, the waiting workers curse because Samuel hurries for no one. They curse until Sam's floppy felt hat is spied coming at the junction, and then a hush settles upon the crowd. They give him lots of room as he shuffles through, for no one wants to be brushed by any part of him, and without glancing left or right he goes directly to the tree with the shoemaker's knife stuck in his belt. He climbs, and holding the dead man close against his breast he cuts the rope and lowers the corpse to the ground. By then it is almost time for the seven o'clock whistle, and before Samuel regains the ground the workers are already in flight down the palm-lined road to the factory, some cursing still, for Samuel has both served and disappointed them. Yet even in their haste they are careful to make room for Samuel as he climbs down, sticks the blade once more in his belt, and shuffles off towards his cottage wordlessly. They all make room for him, and the ones too feeble to work follow at a distance in his wake to lounge beneath the almonds and recount his tale with a mixture of derision and respect.

Stick Song

The early swarm of fireflies was over: only a few darting stragglers were still abroad, winking the solid darkness that stretched and rolled away behind the houses. At a dip in the road they could hear dogs barking from the village on the next hill over. Then drums and voices.

The drums were thick, low, a distant rumble across the quiet valley. The voices were not sweet, yet even at a distance the stick-song chorus made Daaga's skin shiver. For a moment it was like being in a dome with only the drums and naked voices reflecting, and in Daaga an elemental stir to dance erupted despite his nagging fear of dancing: his fear of the feelings stirred and their potential power over him.

He had not heard such music in eight years. He had learned to thrive on the subtleties of Miles Davis, Max Roach; had been many times over stirred by Coltrane and Elvin Jones, but not this way. He had thrown rocks at armed policemen; and armed himself with a new name, a new awareness of his historic enormity he had returned to teach, to awaken the peasant mind from which he had once sought deliverance. Awaken it to its own dormant power.

But did he really know better than them the dimensions of that power? Could economic theory, political awareness, a revised history —could any of these overpower a drum beat?

"Them boys beating good keg," Stone said, "but they can't touch we. . . ."

As the road inclined they could hear the sounds of their village once again, and soon they walked into the tent yard where the men were practicing for carnival. A general noise and bustle blocked out George Village, blocked out the night. Another dome, this one hearty and self-contained, without echo.

"Ah ah, so you come!" the carpenter shuffled forward short and supple, big veins cording his arms and forehead, his face gleaming an enormous smile. So you come! As if some subtle travail by which Daaga was innocently directed had at last succeeded. The carpenter took him by the hand and led him through the thicket of coarse arms, sweat-drenched bodies pressed and humidifying in the electric glare of a naked bulb. Leading him aggressively through the thickened clamor of village men who an hour ago were humble johns or work-wrestled lashleys back-sore and spirit-weary from the unceasing peasant days.

But now!

Now, as if something had dissolved the cagedness around their reserve, it is exuberance, mettle in their voices, an expansive flash to their eyes. As though they not only knew how heart first came to beat, but were the acknowledged substance of its magic. Who under the glare of this one bulb light fluttered by moths and other forage of the night were boasting, arguing, challenging each other, all the while sharing ritual flasks of mountain dew strong still with the vapor of molasses. Homage to king cane. Which with the scent of herbs crushed down where dancing feet had tramped the yard joined an odor that reached away for Daaga. Faint yet persistent, an odor he must have known in the past, pleasantly.

"Aie, aie," the carpenter was gleeful. "Come, come," he said, tugging Daaga through the crowd. "Aie, Conga Man!" the carpenter called as they burst through to a circular space ringed in by the clamor but itself vacant except for one man.

"Aie, Conga Man!"

And from the center of the ring Conga Man watched them approach without replying. In khaki pants and long white shirt untucked, a cricket cap on backwards over a white headband, he hulked at the center of the ring with his chin propped on the tip of his stick.

"This we king," the carpenter said. And Conga Man affected it. The same who to Daaga had been more formally Robert of two bends down the road, husband, father of seven, workman at the factory—now king. Silently awaiting their approach, eyes steady in his concave black face, and red.

"Look Conga Man, look. Is mi boy. Mi boy come!" the carpenter said.

Then Conga Man pulled himself straight, and smiled. "Well Mr. Daaga, you come to play a little stick?"

Daaga wanted to stop himself from grinning but could not. "Just to watch," he said.

"Well we not having much right now, as you could see," Conga Man said.

"I see," Daaga said, looking around.

There were three drums abandoned on the ground, and though several of the men held sticks, the weave of intercourse was syncopal except for a shouting match or two within clusters for the most part engaged in drinking.

"I tell you he woulda come," the carpenter said. Conga Man smiled, his face nevertheless losing no sense of presence. Like a serpent. "I tell all you," the carpenter continued, "from the first day I see him that he was a gentleman, but that he was one a we. You taking a drink Mr. Daaga?"

"But how you mean if he taking a drink?" Conga Man said, accepting the already proferred flask from the beaming carpenter. He took a little to wash his mouth and spray, then a medium swallow. Daaga accepted the flask and did likewise to the carpenter's glee.

"You drink like one a we, man," the carpenter said . . . "Make my heart feel glad." As he completed the triad.

One drummer had returned and now he rattled his skin a little to call the others.

"So you come back from America," Conga Man said. "They does have stick over there?"

"Naah . . ." Daaga replied.

"This the place where stick born!" the carpenter said, doing a quick kalinda step. "You ever hear of Congo Barra? He born right here. This his grandson." Which Conga Man did not deign to acknowledge.

"They used to have stick in my village too," Daaga said.

"Where that?"

"St. Madeleine."

"Yeah. When I was a little boy we used to have stick there too . . ."

"Yes, I know," the carpenter suddenly becoming wise.

The drum rattled, and someone sang—"When ah dead bury mi clothes . . ." Conga Man, leaning once more on his stick rocked back, closed his eyes and smiled.

"I know," the carpenter said. "I used to have a ladyfriend over there, long time before you born. I know they used to have stick. Your own grandfather brother, he was a tiger. But you 'ent know him. He dead before you born. I know they did have stick there, but that before your time."

"I remember carnival days, and the stick-men singing . . ."

"Bois!" an unexpected voice exploded behind Daaga, and he turned to see tall Mr. Gray dancing before Conga Man, his empty fingers rigid, circling the air like some wrestler's. "Bois!" Mr. Gray lunged at Conga Man, who ducked and came up in time to catch the older man in his arms. The two men embraced and laughed full in each other's faces.

"Gray," the carpenter called, "look Mr. Daaga."

And Gray turned slowly to survey, an unsmiling scrutiny but not unkind. "So. Mr. Daaga you come to pass some time with the boys," he said.

"A little bit."

"I just telling him," the carpenter said, "I just telling him this the place where stick born." And old Gray nodded his head in concurrence, without taking his eyes off Daaga.

"But his grandfather village had one or two good stick-men too, you know."

"Oh yes? Who his grandfather?" Mr. Gray asked.

"Old man Grant, used to pastor that Baptist church outside Usine."

Mr. Gray's eyes narrowed, then his frown relaxed as though he had just solved a problem. "Is so? Boy," he said to Daaga, "you a Grant?"

Daaga smiled. "The old man was my grandfather."

"Who you for—one of his daughters or his son?"

"His son."

"And how you 'ent carrying the name?"

Daaga smiled.

"I've been saying to myself all this time," Mr. Gray announced at large, "I know this man's blood." And back to Daaga, "I used to court one of your tanties, boy."

"He 'ent know 'bout that," the carpenter said. "That before he born." And turning to Daaga asked, "When you went to America Mr. Daaga? What time it was when you leave Trinidad?"

"Nineteen-fifty-eight."

"And you 'ent come back till this year?"

"That's right."

Again the drums rattled, and someone raised "Sergeant Brown calling mi name . . ." but he did not get a chorus. As Mr. Gray returned to scrutinizing.

"Young fella," he finally asked with force, "you know where you get that name?"

To which Daaga smiled, "Sure." Never forgetting how he had self-consciously selected it from the dusty shelves of a North American library, at a time when many like himself had begun to renew, reaffirm, reconstitute the black African in their person. "Sure."

"Hmm," Gray grunted. "Daaga was a hell of a man, you know. Where the bottle?"

"Yes," Daaga said. Wondering however did old unlettered Gray, back villager that he was had come to know anything about the first Daaga.

They drank and Gray went on. "How you get the name, somebody give you or you pick it up yourself?"

"I picked it out," Daaga said. And it should have been pleasant encountering another who knew of and obviously respected the first Daaga, but it wasn't.

"That's what I'm saying," Gray's voice was almost amused, "Because only few people in Trinidad know anything about Daaga. Where you get it, in America?"

"Yes."

"You see!" cried Gray, announcing once more to the crowd at large, "America 'ent only for making money—you getting history there too, man. History."

And how did the history of that first Daaga ever come to old Gray's attention?

"When you know, you know." Gray spoke like one privy to a mystery, and Daaga offered him a smile, hoping to ignite some feeling of kinship, comradeship, some contact beyond the mere breath of their voices. But the old man's eyes would not let him in.

"You ever hear about Daaga?" Gray said pompously to the carpenter.

"No. But the name sound like a stick-man to me."

"Stick-man! Daaga was a warrior! In the eighteenth century when the Spanish still keeping slaves, Daaga turned on them. Man, look! Right there in St. Joseph, oui! And if it wasn't for a kiss-mi-ass traitor he woulda take over this whole island. Yes! The whole island. But the traitor betray him. And when they bring him out to shoot him, he turn his backside gi them, man. They want to see him look sorry and hang-dog, but he turn his back gi them as if to say 'Kiss my ass!' You think they know what to do with that?"

"He must've been a bold man."

"He was a tough man."

"Anybody with a name like that bound to be dangerous. You going up?"

They drank and the flask was empty.

"Kiss mi ass, he tell them," Gray said, pursuing the story or history of that first Daaga with emphasis, as if at one time he might have taken such a name himself, handled such deeds himself.

"Where you get all that Gray?" the carpenter asked.

"The priest."

"What priest, that maracòn at the Presbyterian?"

"I'm telling you, man," Gray spoke with forbearance, "these Americans 'ent stupid like all you think."

"What that priest know about Daaga or anything in Trinidad?"

"Them Americans know everything, man. They smart too bad. You 'ent hear this Mr. Daaga here say that where he get his name?"

"That priest only have a lot of books."

"That's knowledge!" Gray's voice rose like a drum clout. "Knowledge!"

Then the drummers were reassembled, and the heavy keg picked up a heartbeat. A strong, steady, muffled beat.

"Book knowledge ain't no kind of knowledge," someone said.

"How about the lost books of the Bible," Gray came back vigorously. "You imagine what is in them?"

The light drum cut into the deep-toned keg, and soon the third drum picked up a second off-rhythm, until together they were sounding memories which caused Daaga to rock with a smile on his face.

All talk trailed to an end.

Conga Man, eyes closed, aloof, slowly raised his arms above his head, stick pointing to the sky. Daaga, Gray, the carpenter, they all moved back leaving Conga alone in the circle. A voice raised—

"My mama gon pay the bail

Don' let me sleep in the royal jail . . ."

and several immediately chorused—

"Tell the sergeant

Mi mamma gon' pay the bail . . ."

Conga Man began his dance. He leaped in the air, arms outstretched, to land softly on his toes and stalk the circle like a panther wrathfully in search of prey. The cutting drum saluted. Conga weaved, flicking his stick to a defensive position, then abruptly he stood rock still, a challenge to any who dared attack. An agony in his stance, but forever belligerent. Vulnerable he may be, but fearless, and with a price for whoever would find out.

In between the drums a singer chanted his call again, and the chorus answered. Like liquid memory the vibrating beat quivered Daaga's belly and arms, his feet. Aroused to an anciently imbedded dance, he wanted to leap like Conga, stomp the earth, bend the sky. A tremor of fearlessness electrified him.

"You want to play?" the carpenter shouted in his ear above the drums and singing. And Gray was still looking at him, an intensely neutral scrutiny.

Daaga only smiled. When uneasiness, when fear is conquered, man carries out the eternal with nothing but ease. Daaga only smiled.

All the men singing, their voices came sweet. Several danced, though taking care not to confront Conga where he was planted shimmying, his stick crossed and ready. They danced around him, beside him, in complement to his contained power, but never confronting him. The drums rumbled and clapped like sweet thunder, and when Daaga closed his eyes they pounded right in deep beneath his skin and massaged his viscera, so that a power steamed from his head distinct as the smell of sweat, fresh earth, crushed leaves, and something didn't have a name but was bright and blue in color. Deepening to black in moments. A discovery of peace in terror. Demon, benevolent, brave martyr, but above all fearless; at work, peace, or play, fearless; divided, conquered, fearlessly emerging, reassembling, dominating; fearless. Daaga sang with the chorus, rocked his head and bounced where he stood; but waited for himself to calm down.

Then with a flourish the drums came down and the song ended. The men went back to palaver and drinking, several thrusting flasks towards Conga, who, once more pleasant and benign, shook the sweat from around his eyes, joined in the laughter, and drank.

"How you like the boys?" Stone asked, materializing before Daaga. "They good?"

"Yes, yes . . ."

"I did tell you so. I see they make you hot too," Stone grinned, "little bit again and you would've jumped in, right?"

To which Daaga could smile and say, "This music is sweeter than anything I've heard in a long time."

"I tell you though," Stone confided, "if you get hot and want to jump in, don't take on Conga Man. He's very dangerous . . ."

To which Daaga smiled. "Who should I take on, you?"

"Who, me. I don't play stick. I don't want nobody busting my head open." Stone lifting his hat to stroke his head. "This coconut good just as it is and it gon' stay that way till I get to New York. Only way I get mi head buss is if a New York police hit me in a riot . . ."

To which Daaga smiled, relaxed now. Maybe one day Stone would find a library—perhaps the very one Daaga had known—and reemerge with a new name. Then his cultivating Daaga would have been worth it. But again, he might just get lost on Brooklyn Avenue. There was no way Daaga could prepare him for all he would encounter even living the way they did as brothers before his departure.

Maybe one day he would come back with something more than the bravado of a big city street corner. To this same village, and be just the finite dream of his ancestors incarnate.

The rum was new and a little bit smoky, but it drank well. The men praised the hand that made it. They talked . . . the babble of men in good spirits because of knowing that weakness and fear would sometime before the gathering broke be exorcised, and they would live sharing the vision. They talked, until the talk divided itself between just two and the others listened. Old Gray's voice shrieked to make a lion pause. "Daaga is a wicked name, oui!"

The other fell like frozen sand on the ear—"I don't believe none of that stupidness . . ." And Crazy Desmond's eyes looked sharp with contempt.

"Is a wicked name ah telling you . . ."

"So what it got in that—my name ent wicked too?"

"You? Go on! You ever start a revolution? You ever tell white man kiss your ass? You gon stand up like a man when they point the gun at you? A chicken like you . . ."

"So ah is chicken: a chicken fowl-cock! Well buss mi head, nuh! Look it dey—buss it. Ah is chicken. Well get a stick—ah want to see you buss chicken head . . ."

"Damn Trinidadian so blasted stupid, you can't tell them nothing. Where a stick . . . ?"

A waiting voice raised the song again—

"Mi mamma gon pay the bail

Mi mamma gon pay the bail

Tell the sergeant

Mi mamma gon pay the bail . . ."

and the drums overtook the melody—

Buh gu duk/Buh gu duk . . .

And Daaga, Mr. Daaga, relaxed now. Another rum: the drums. And uncontrollably out of context the memory of himself on a toilet seat in Idylwild. It is a mountain resort in Southern California U.S.A., flat board cabins between the rustic redwood trees, and the company of a brown woman. It is the summer season, with a blue sky, golden sun, high in the desert atmosphere, and bronze-blonde teenagers everywhere eager for experiments to exploit the vulnerabilities ordinarily buttoned down below. It is a porthole toilet: the "closet" of an earlier childhood. With the sun striated through waving fir branches in a sky blue, deep and eternal. What is it? What is it being sucked into a solitude above the world, becoming pure?

What is it—being sucked into the solitude of ephemeral darkness which yet echoes a voice, a warmth, arms clasping.

On the barren ground of an idle hilltop it is the lover embracing his mate beneath the silhouette of empty avocado trees and many unmoved stars in the distance, saying Call my name I want to hear you call my name I want to hear you call my name. And even farther than the stars across the treetops, the ocean washes languidly alike for lovers, dead fish or the melancholy seaman laying down his seine.

All women were one. For a fleeting uncontrollable moment he missed Woman, mermaid of the liquid night. And in a moment resolved to the excruciating sweetness of their future embrace.

Another rum: the drums.

And Daaga, Mr. Daaga, dancing like an ancient warrior before his totem. With a stick in his hand, and the dance coming easily. So that his nostrils burned, and the bones of his face could feel the atmosphere. Daaga dancing in the one-bulb electric light, and the men making room for him, backing off into the traditional circle where it is the drummers, himself, and in a corner the hole where the blood for each night is collected. Daaga dancing. Leaping as lithe as Conga Man on his toes, and the drums filled on dew from the mount following him everywhere, commenting, instructing, sometimes compelling his motion.

The drums tell you what to do.

"Aie, but look, the American dancing!"

"He ent no American: he's a born Trinidadian."

"Aie, but he dancing sweet, man."

"Bound to. No Yankee could dance this dance. Besides, he Daaga."

"Who that?"

"The fella what did kill all the Spanish and them before your grandfather time."

"He come back? He spirit come back?"

"Spirit like that don't bury, you know . . ."

Buh gu duk/Buh gu duk . . .

"Aie ah aie! Ah go buss a head tonight! Tonight, tonight!"

It is Crazy Desmond: in his ten-dollar shirt with the cuffs rolled back, sharkskin pants, alligator shoes, and a brims-up felt hat on his head. Dancing left foot, right foot, marking the ground with his stick. For a second, Daaga would have melted into the night, flowed on back to being idle and wild. But Desmond's scent enveloped him like a woman's perfume edged with a touch of rawness, and behind his back the drums rained thunder from a peak. In his right eye Conga Man stood judiciously, his stick grounded like a staff between his legs; and before him Desmond played his stick like an obeah-man jabbing spirits, then prepared a carré.

Daaga heard the drums inside his head. He danced. Before him Desmond stretched and retracted like a cobra, his stick cocked above his head. Daaga danced: then planted his feet and took a stance. Immediately there came a blur between his eyes and a knocking dullness. In a single voice the men roared. They broke the circle, and several rushed by him to hug Desmond. The blood was warm coming down his face, as Conga Man led him over to the hole and forced him to bend his head over it. Stone's voice said, "But all you wicked, oui! All you let Desmond cut the man?"

The rum bath brought a sting to his forehead. His vision came instantly sharper, as did his ears, so that all around him slowed down, and from the core of an impenetrable calm he waited while they worked on stopping the blood.

"He ent cut bad," said Conga Man.

"But he coulda get his eye dig out!" Stone said. "The man come quite from New York, and all you let him jump in here to get his head buss!"

"Well why you didn't get a stick and stand up then, eh?"

"Me ent tell nobody I is stick-man. But all you let Desmond take advantage man."

"Take advantage, what? When time come, jackass have to bray. Besides, Daaga or whoever his name is ain't from New York. He from right here."

"Yes. And I believe he gon cut Desmond good, good," Conga Man said. "You'll see. If Desmond didn't swinging sideways stick he done cut already!"

"You ent see the way Daaga measure him with his eye?"

"I tell you, Desmond done cut already."

"He gon take him on again."

And in the old days it was terrifying to watch the grown men play. Terrifying to hear their challenges, then see the fierceness on one face turn to blood. Chilling, the vision of dominance and humility in a dance that always ended the same; chilling, the odor of fear when a man knew he was going to be bled, the lust in the eyes of the bleeder. As a child Daaga had cried for weeks on the vision of losers struck down. But tonight he was quite calm.

It would have been better if there were a song of his own. He was going to cut Desmond tonight, and it would have been nice if he had a song to which this verse could be added. Daaga made a mental note to compose one. The cut between his eyes was dressed, and someone had put a petit-quart of the clear rum in his hand. He raised stick and rum above his head and a few men cheered. He did not turn immediately to look for Desmond.

Not too deep in his past it is daylight saving time in Los Angeles, and the town is on fire. Black men women and children on rampage in the streets, harvesting their due from foreign businesses, dancing a bloody ballet to the rat-a-tat of National Guard fire. And at curtain call nobody knows how many dead, God alone how many left wounded, but no mourning. No applause, no mourning, only an argument left between the wrong and the wronged, into which she could not but induct him, falling back into his life suddenly after all the cha cha chas and bossa novas he had spent in quest of a true lady companion asking What are you going to do about it? As if that were indeed a question! Challenging him on the mount in Griffith Park, Haven't you thought about it? Two brown legs smooth, unyielding, resolved to the honey arms of Lady Satin Bellamy from Baton Rouge —never mind the weekends as companion in Beverly Hills—breathing in his ear the native promise everyone knows is but a dream; which nevertheless bears him away promising, promising, promising. What are you going to do? she had asked, Aren't you scared? From the mount in Griffith Park, looking down on a pastel world one corner of which billowed black smoke.

The drums began again, and a chantrèlle raised the lávwé—
"Mamma look ah 'fraid
  Mamma look ah 'fraid the demon . . ."
and got an immediate chorus
  "Mamma look ah 'fraid
  No stick-man don't 'fraid no demon . . ."
Daaga swallowed and handed back the empty petit-quart. He wiped his stick, burnishing the metal cap on its end, then he prepared to pit. The drums rumbled, the circle re-formed. The drums climbed; he started a slow dance. And there was Desmond: leaping tall already, swaying, and retracting. Daaga watched him steadily. They circled. Desmond feinted once, twice. They circled again, then Desmond charged, Daaga saw all clearly: and although Desmond was swift Daaga gave ground evading the blow, then brought his own heavily down upon Desmond's skull a split second before their two bodies crashed together.

It was a mighty roar from the men, someone screaming distinctly, "Oh God! He kill him!" But Desmond was not dead. On the ground his eyes were glazed, and before friends could remove his hat blood ran from beneath it freely down his left temple. They lifted him and without any help from his legs dragged him to the blood hole. The drums played sweet thunder, then broke, and Daaga found himself lifted in the air by many hands.

The men, elated, Conga Man among them, leaped and shouted. They talked aloud in each others' faces and in short time reached consensus Daaga was too rare a phenomenon. When last did anyone see stick play like that? When last did anyone see balance, brains, and fearlessness like that? It was too much for the village to contain that night, and like a compulsive fire going forward they commandeered the four cars resident in the village, crammed into them singing fresh songs, and set out to show, to share this rare phenomenon in George Village across the hills, or any other where men may leave the safety of their homes and come out in the night to see, to challenge this new hero—Daaga. Behind they left Crazy Desmond sitting under the one bulb light still dazed, with a friend or two feeding him rum, shaving the hair from around his wound to lay a patch on it.